Lock Down Publications and Ca$h
Presents

TENDER 2

Slice of the Devil's Pie

Written By

Khufu

First Edition 2025

Printed in the United States of America

Lock Down Publications
P.O. Box 944
Stockbridge, GA 30281
www.lockdownpublications.com

Like our page on Facebook: Lock Down Publications
www.facebook.com/lockdownpublications.ldp

Stay Connected with Us!

Text **LOCKDOWN** to 22828 to stay up-to-date with new releases, sneak peaks, contests and more…

Like our page on Facebook:
Lock Down Publications

Join Lock Down Publications/The New Era Reading Group

Visit our website:
www.lockdownpublications.com

Follow us on Instagram:
Lock Down Publications

Email Us: We want to hear from you!

Acknowledgements

First off, all praises to the Almighty life force that flows through all living things! Without you...nothing is tangible, and I am in perpetuity! We are all born with purpose and some of talent...to never find one's purpose would be shear atrophy, and I have blessed to be able to demonstrate my creative suavity prolifically through novelizing and music. To my fans...your loyalty is appreciated beyond measure! Ca$h and LDP it's all love! To Michelle...I love you! Your loyalty remains unmatched! Free the guys S.M.M 45 World Wide! Ola Ken Da Blazer! A.M.G Kreon! 210 Slick, YSW Worldd, CC, Truth, and them Frontlinerz! It's all love! Dead or alive...I remain top ten in this novel world...I stand on that!

Rest in power: Stacey, Tela, Tayda, Lanetta, Man Man, Ponyboy, Krazy E, Toby, Tayda Bread & Kody

Free Da Real: Quentin Bradley, Killa Scrab, Jimmy Reeves, Vamp, C-Rock, Tre Plus, Keedy, Junx from Trinidad & Jermey

Dedication

I dedicate this book to my son Aj! I love you son!

Quote:

"You can only hate someone whom you have the capacity to love…"

Chapter 2
Stand On Business

When Face stepped outside of the courtroom, he inhaled and exhaled deeply. It felt as if he were breathing a different type of oxygen... way purer than the recycled air he'd been inhaling for a year.

"Mr. Williams, it's been a pleasure working your case. Hopefully you never need me again, but if so, I look forward to it."

"Hold up, man! What the fuck was in them folders?" Face implored.

Mr. Williams stopped in front of an all-red twenty-twenty-five K5, then turned to face Face.

"Everything you wanna know will be answered in here," Johnny Cochran assured, shaking Face's hand before walking off.

Moments later, the passenger window rolled down.

"Wass poppin, Damu?" a voice implored from inside the vehicle.

Face peered inside and saw that it was Assata in the backseat with Shooter, and Lil Fif God in the front. Face opened the back door and climbed inside.

"Niggaz like us!" Face retorted, bumping B's with Assata.

"Already! You know the vibe. Listen, I know yo mind spinnin' like a muthafucka right nah, so let me put you on O-fifty. Yo big fool, Kream hit me up and asked me if I had any reach in the system. When he informed me that it was you, I had my people do they lil one-two. You owe me one too, homie," Assata declared, handing Face a folder that looked identical to the one Johnny Cochran handed the judge.

"Pull off, Shooter," Assata demanded, sparking a blunt.

Face opened the folder and noted pictures of Judge Mora and Lapointe snorting coke and having sex with underage girls. There was also a note that stated: **"I HAVE FOOTAGE TOO!!!"**

Assata had retrieved this dirt from Ketta, her stepmother.

"Damn, that's brayz! Dem krakaz be doin' the most behind closed doors, but'll take a nigga life hollin' 'bout a menace to society," Face added.

"I got footage of them krakaz all at Diddy freak-offs and all," Assata mentioned.

"So why you ain't use this info to free Kream?"

"Kream ain't catch no time. Five years ain't shit, homie. You needed it, or you wooda neva seen the light of day," she explained.

"I feel you. And whateva you need from me, I'm on it!" Face assured.

"Oh, I know," Assata retorted, somewhat as a threat.

She grabbed the folder and handed Face the blunt as they pulled into The Carter apartments — the same ones he lived in with KoKo.

"Listen! I advise you to stop fuckin' wit' that hoe who gotchu jammed. I will not be using my resources for that bullshit again. Nah... I got'cha apartment back, the same one you had. Anything that had of yours is hers now. Start over, homie."

Shooter and Lil Fif God exited the vehicle and opened Assata's door.

"Two-twelve, Damu!" Assata pronounced, bumping B's with Face before getting out.

Face got out behind her, and moments later Lil Fif God threw him the keys to the K5 and the apartment.

14

"This yo whip, homie. I'ma bark at'chu later," Assata pronounced, heading to a Benz truck that had been following them the whole time.

"Damn, this Kia bloody as fuck," Face thought to himself. "I need ya math, Bloody!" Face shouted.

"You already got it!" she retorted before hopping in the back seat of the truck.

Face watched the truck duck off in traffic before heading up to his apartment. Once he entered, he noted that everything — from sofas to appliances — was red. Moments later, a phone began to ring in the kitchen. Face followed the sound and found a Galaxy on the table. He picked it up and answered.

"Yeah?"

"I told ju, you already got the math," Assata asserted, chuckling.

"You are appreciated, Bloody," Face retorted, placing the roach from the blunt in a red ashtray that was on a red oak table.

"Woooooop!" Assata hummed before hanging up.

Face moved through the rest of the apartment and saw that it was fully furnished — both rooms and the bathroom. He even had a new wardrobe with kicks to match each outfit, and two FN Five-seven by twenty-eight millimeter pistols sitting on the closet floor.

"Nah, that's how a nigga suppose to come home," he yelled out in excitement, then noticed two duffel bags on his bed.

Face quickly approached them and unzipped them. It was ten cans in each bag, with a note inside that read:

We married nah, homie! I want fifty twenty's apiece! Stand on bidness or get stood over!— Assata

Face smiled, shaking his head side to side. He didn't take kindly to threats but found this one amusing. *Why would she roll out the red carpet for me and threaten to kill me in the same breath?*

Awl, maan! She wana real one, Face believed in his mind.

***

After washing the federal stench from his flesh, Face grabbed both pistols and hopped in his K5, dipped in Amiri. He push-started the whip, then sat in silence for a moment, basking in the thought of really being free. His phone ringing interrupted his moment.

"Yeah?" Face answered, putting the car in drive and pulling off.

"How that air taste out there, Bloody?"

Face smiled, knowing that voice by sound.

"Kream! Wass poppin, five?"

"You already know! Niggaz like us!" Kream retorted.

"All the time! Damn, Bloody, it's good to be barkin' wit'chu."

"Likewise, homie. Listen, I'm sho' Assata po'ed you a drink on how you at, where you at."

"I mean, she laced me a lil piece, but she ain't po' me a drank on why she did it for you. You hittin' that?" Face implored, chuckling.

Kream laughed too, but turned serious moments later.

"Nall, I ain't touch that, that's the homie. It was more of a favor-fo-a-favor type bituation, ya hear me? She needed somethin' handled behind the G-wall, and I stood on that. In exchange, she agreed to free you, but she still gon' want somethin' from you too though, homie. So just be O-fifty when she ball you, ya hear me?"

"Fasho," Face pronounced.

He pulled back up on 23rd with B3 in tow. Both exited the vehicle and walked up to B3's mom's spot, where she was perched in a lawn chair.

"Hey, Mama Duke," Face greeted, giving her a kiss on the cheek.

"Oh, my God! Is that who I think it is?" she questioned, her face lighting up.

"Yes, ma'am, it's me. You lookin' good," Face responded sincerely.

"Boy, I heard you was doin' life! Lord have mercy. Come here, give me a hug," Mama Duke requested.

Face smiled and gave her a big hug, lifting her up off her feet.

"You done grew into a whole man now. I remember when you was runnin' around here wit' snot in yo' nose. And look at you now!"

"Yes, ma'am," Face replied with a chuckle.

B3 smiled, happy to see the two reunite.

"Boy, don't you leave without comin' to see me, ya hear?" Mama Duke warned.

"Yes, ma'am. I wouldn't dare," Face assured.

As the two men walked inside, B3 closed the door behind them.

"Boy, Mama love you, mane," B3 uttered, smirking.

"Always have," Face returned.

The two sat down on the couch. Face immediately scanned the room, the walls filled with family pictures and graduation photos of B3's stepkids.

"So, whatchu really tryna do, mane?" B3 asked.

"I need some fire power. Somethin' small I can tote daily, and somethin' big for when it get heavy. You know who got what?"

B3 rubbed his beard.

"Yeah, mane. My lil' cousin got them thangs. He stay in Brown Sub. We can spin ova there right now if you want."

"Say less. Let's slide," Face insisted.

***

Within twenty minutes, Face and B3 pulled up to a ragged duplex in Brown Sub. Kids were running around outside while loud music blasted from a parked Chevy Caprice.

B3's cousin, Rico, came outside shirtless, his tattoos covering his chest.

"What it do, cuh?" Rico greeted, dapping B3.

"This my nigga Face," B3 introduced.

"Wassup, homie?" Rico nodded.

"Shit, chillin'. B3 said you might got somethin' I need," Face got straight to it.

Rico smirked, then motioned for them to follow him inside.

The house smelled of loud weed and fried chicken grease. Rico opened a duffel bag on the table, pulling out a Glock nineteen and a chopped SKS with a folding stock.

"This what I got on deck right now. Both clean."

Face picked up the Glock nineteen, racking it back.

"How much you taxin'?" Face asked.

"Four for the baby, eight for the SK," Rico replied.

Face reached in his pocket and peeled off twelve hundred in cash without hesitation.

"Both mine," Face declared.

"Bet. You want some extra clips?" Rico offered.

"Yeah. Load me up."

Within minutes, Face left the spot strapped and ready for war.

***

Later that night, Face sat alone in his whip outside KoKo's mama house, chain-smoking back-to-back Newports. He could see G-Man still on the porch with two of his niggaz.

Face's trigger finger itched. His chest rose and fell heavy as he debated on hopping out. He gripped the Glock tight, then loosened his hold, his mind running a hundred miles an hour.

Patience, nigga... timing everything, he told himself, finally cranking up the whip and pulling off into the night.

"Listen, homie, I'm glad to see you back out here! I'on know how you came from up under that, but that's the past. We finna get this money in the present."

"Hold up, partna," Face interjected smoothly, putting the back of his hand on Moses' chest.

"Look me up on Pacer. Before we do bidness, check my paperwork out. Homie, I'm lightweight tired of hearing that shit," Face voiced calmly, then hit the blunt.

"Nawl, it ain't nothin' like that, family. I know you solid! I just meant that God was wit'chu. I'll neva come at'chu like that, you trippin', my nigga," Moses corrected.

"I hear you. Wassup, though?" Face questioned, passing the blunt back to Moses.

"I got twenty P's for you. Just give me a stack apiece," Moses told 'em.

"What it is?"

"Runts! Straight pressure," Moses boasted, flicking the roach on the pavement.

"I call that," Face accepted.

"Aight, I got 'em in the garage. Listen, I wanna ask you somethin', though."

Face looked Moses in his eyes.

"Wassup?" Face implored, folding his arms across his chest.

"You still fuckin' wit' KoKo?"

"Come on, man. Hell fuck nawl!"

"Okay," Moses retorted, shaking his head in approval. "Fam, from me to you... you a real solid nigga. Everybody ain't meant to be around you. Everybody don't deserve yo' energy. In life, it's levels. It's levels to life, and sometimes you gotta leave a muthafucka at that low level and transcend to that level you know you s'posed to be vibrating on. All

19

that givin' bitches a chance who you know don't deserve it is a dubb. That shit is a waste of time, and I'm sho' I'm pullin' yo' coat on some shit that you already know."

Face listened assiduously, feeling every word Moses was dropping.

"I'm only tellin' you this kuz I fuck wit'cha, fam."

"Shit deep," Face added.

"Yeah, I done been there, fam. A bitch can have the most flamin' mouth and pussy in the world… but when the shit be toxic, it ain't nothin' but a slice of the Devil's pie, homie," Moses voiced.

Listening to Moses talk caused Face to have flashes of all the deadly and toxic moments he had with KoKo. Realizing how foolish he'd been making himself look, he felt as if he was having a sucka attack. Face quickly composed himself and got down to bidness.

"I feel you, bra. I'm focused, nah let's get to it," Face stated.

***

Later on that night, around 8:35 p.m., Face said his goodbyes and told B3 that it was time to hit it. Once to his car, World called out to Face and made his way toward him.

"Bra, wassup? Let's hit the club," World proposed, hyped up.

Face pondered the idea for a moment.

"I'on know, bra. I really wanted to just lay back in my shit and relax… like I'm really free, my nigga. A nigga want a lil' time to his self," Face explained.

"Maaan! Fuck you wanna be in the house for, after bein' locked down for over a year? You can get some alone time when you leave the club. Shid, if I was you, I'll be tryin' to fuck somethin'," World added.

Face looked at B3.

"What'chu wanna do, B3?"

"Shid, I'm wit' you, mane."

"Maan! Everything on me!" World pronounced, going in his pocket and handing Face a stack. "Where you stayin' at?"

"I got my spot back on 25th at the Carter," Face informed.

"Aight, bet. I'ma pull up 'round 11:30. Me and TJ," World asserted before spinning off.

Face and B3 hopped in the K5 and got in the wind.

"So, wassup, 3?"

"How you mean, mane?" B3 implored.

"You gettin' money?"

"I do a lil' somethin'. Sometimes, I go cut grass wit' my folks, or I might do a lil' roofing, mane. Why wassup? You need a job, mane?"

Face laughed at B3's gesture.

"Nawl, homie. I ain't workin' for no kraka. I asked you that to see if you wanna get some money. I'on trust nobody, my nigga, and you been rockin' out wit' me," Face voiced.

"Mane, hell yeah I want some money, mane. What we talkin', mane?" B3 asked as Face pulled on the side of the road in front of B3's girl's public housing apartment. Face popped the trunk.

"Look, homie. Grab one of them duffel bags out my trunk. It's ten cans in there. Give me two bands apiece, homie," Face proclaimed, watching his surroundings.

"What's in the cans, mane?"

"Ten pounds of Runts. Straight pressure, homie," Face pronounced, grabbing his strap and placing it on his lap.

He noted the crowd of niggaz down the street in KoKo's mother's yard looking in their direction.

"I got'cha, mane. I appreciate that, mane," B3 said, dapping Face up and pulling the FN from his britches to hand back to him.

"Nah, homie, that's you now. Make sho' you brang it wit'chu when we hit the club."

"Fasho, mane! I'll be ready when you pull up, mane," B3 assured, stepping out of the whip.

He grabbed a duffel, then headed inside. Face pulled off, creeping behind five percent tint. When he slid past KoKo's mother's house, G-Man and his homies were outside. Some were carelessly slipping while others were on point, clutching their weapons. Face smiled behind the tint as he crept on by.

"I'ma get'chu, tough-ass nigga," Face mumbled to himself.

Chapter 3
Yes Ma'am!

Face had doubled back to his apartment for something to smoke, hit J-n-J's for two bottles of Remy, then made his way to the graveyard that was on enemies turf. He parked on the side of the road on 12th Street and left the car running.

"I'm finna go pay my respect to the dead," Face proclaimed, handing B3 one of his pistols.

They grabbed a few blunts, a bottle a piece, and hopped out chest out, chin up. Face made his way to his lil cousin Bloody J's grave and lit a blunt. B3 lit his blunt and held the FN by his side watching everything.

"Damn, fam. You letta a nigga stop ya lil clock, huh?" Face inquired, popping the seal to the Remy bottle and pouring some over J's grave.

He took a sip then squatted low to the earth as if this method would surely allow J to hear him better. B3 popped his bottle, took a sip, then placed it on the ground, still watching his surroundings.

"Don't trip though, I spanked that boy. He in the dirt wit'chu a few plots down," Face announced impassively.

He took another sip then hit his blunt again.

"Bleed in peace, fam." Face stood, poured more liquor on J's grave, then headed to another grave a little further down.

When he made it to Kierra's grave, he seen that a fresh bouquet of flowers had been placed to the right of the tombstone.

23

"Wassup pornstar? I miss you, girl. I know you tossin' in yo grave sayin', 'Nigga I told ju bout fuckin' wit' that hoe,'" Face mocked as a single tear fell from his right eye. "Some people just love who they love, and it take certain bituations and circumstances to sho' you that, that person ain't for you," Face explained, taking another shot.

"Tighten up, we got company, mane," B3 announced, flicking the roach in the air and putting one in the head of his FN.

"Gotta go, ma," Face pronounced, kissing Kierra's tombstone before rising with his bottle in one hand and pistol in the other.

"Aye! Who the fuck that is wit' all that dead on, kuz?" a lil nigga yelled out of a pack of niggaz standing on the side of a Tahoe.

He was referring "dead" to the color red that Face had on.

"I can't hear you lil nigga, pull up!" Face yelled as him and B3 inched closer to them for a perfect shot.

"I said—"

"Hold up!" a tall nigga that had braids with beads on the end yelled, stepping out of the Tahoe. "Face, boy that's you?"

Face and B3 walked right up to the crowd still clutching.

"C-Rock, boy wass poppin'?" Face implored, mugging the lil nigga who questioned his colors.

"Y'all boys stand down!" C-Rock ordered his lil niggaz.

Face and C-Rock had done time together in prison and even crushed some out-of-towners together for the sake of putting the city on the map in the prison system.

"It's good to see you, baby, but what'chu doin' on this side? Pistol all out and shit," said C-Rock, who was an O.G. from 13th Street.

"My people buried over here, my nigga! As for this pistol, it's a part of my attire, homie," Face explained, with B3 beside him ready to demonstrate. "Anything else?" Face implored.

24

"Nall, homie, you good. Come see ya people anytime," C-Rock pronounced.

"Facts!" Face stated with murder in his eyes and on his mind.

"What about'chu, lil nigga? You straight?" Face asked Joseph, who was the one asking about his colors.

Joseph sucked his teeth before replying.

"Maaan!" Joseph started but was cut off by C-Rock.

"Yeah, listen to ya big homie, lil nigga," Face advised before heading to his whip, jumping in and pulling off.

***

It was a little after 2:00 p.m. when Face pulled up to his mother's house. The atmosphere was boisterous and polluted with loud weed and liquor. Never seeing the K5 before, World snatched out an AR pistol and made his way towards the unknown vehicle. His lil homie TJ grabbed his Saint Victor pistol that shot 5.56 NATO rounds and made his way towards the back of the whip.

"Aye, stop playin' wit deez niggaz, mane," B3 advised, clutching the FN Face had given him.

Face chuckled sinisterly then popped his door open. He stepped out clutching his FN.

"What'chu lil niggas wanna do!" Face implored with a huge smirk on his face.

World's expression went from deadly to pure shock and confusion.

"Da fuck! Face?" World questioned, looking at Face, up at his people who were on the porch, then back at his brother.

"You know what it is, nigga! I'm back out'chere! Nah, either shoot me or salute me!" Face pronounced.

TJ smiled, happy to see Face. TJ was World's childhood friend from down the street.

"Damn, nigga, everybody thought you was facing life and shit! Wass poppin', nigga?" World implored, bumpin' B's with Face.

"Us, never them," Face retorted.

"Nigga, you ain't hit nobody up and let us know nothin'! What'chu—you beat a body and a attempt?"

"Yea, carjackin' too. I'ma lace you later!" Face assured.

"Boy, we almost totaled this pretty ass rental," World disclosed, laughing.

"This ain't no rental," Face informed, waving for B3 to get out of the car. "I had my shooter lerkin too, nah," he stated as B3 stepped out and tucked the FN in his Palm Angels.

World chuckled.

"What's up wit it, 3?" World asked.

"Wassup, mane? I told this nigga not to play wit'chu niggaz, mane," B3 proclaimed, shaking his head.

"I'm tryin' to tell'em," World added.

"Wassup, big homie?" TJ spoke, dapping Face up.

He wasn't gang bangin', but he was on go when it came to World.

"Wass poppin'," Face replied.

"I know that ain't who I think it is!" Pandora yelled after stepping out onto her front porch and seeing her son.

"You better believe it!" Face retorted, tucking his pistol and heading towards his mother.

"Oh my God! Thank you Jesus!" Pandora yelled, hugging Face's neck while tears streamed down her face.

"I love you, ma," Face pronounced as he felt his mother's entire body trembling.

"Love you too, son."

"I know that ain't my brother!" Sierra screamed, stepping out of the garage and running towards Face.

When she reached him she wrapped her arms around him and their mother.

"What up, sis?"

"All maan, this shit got me crying, man," Sierra disclosed, wiping the tears from her face.

"Yeah, that boy back out here," World added excitedly.

Everybody who attended the get together began to clap and cheer loudly. The atmosphere was so emotional that people were wiping tears from their faces, including B3.

"Come inside. I wanna talk to you about something," Pandora pronounced, pulling Face by his hand.

"Aight ma. I'm fuck wit' y'all after I talk wit' mama," Face told everybody.

He followed his mother inside, and she pulled him into her room, closing the door behind them.

"I'm so glad you home," Pandora stated happily.

"Me too, ma."

Pandora's face expression changed as she got serious.

"Nah, I'm yo' mama. I wont'chu to tell me the truth."

"Yes ma'am."

"Did you kill that boy and tried to kill KoKo too?"

Face looked his mother in the eyes and answered her.

"Yes ma'am. I tried to kill both of them," he admitted shamelessly.

Pandora looked her son in the eyes, seeing him for what he really was for the first time. She inhaled deeply and exhaled slowly, shaking her head in understanding.

"Okay. Always let me know what's goin' on wit'chu. Okay?"

"Yes ma'am."

"Is you done with that girl?"

"Yeah, that's over wit," Face retorted, not convincingly.

Pandora gazed at him then got up to go grab something from her dresser. She turned around and handed Face an envelope addressed to him with no sender.

"What this is?" he asked, opening the envelope.

Pandora shrugged her shoulders. When he opened it, it appeared to be a letter. He glanced at his mother before reading it.

Dear Face,

I know the last person you wanna hear from is me, but I'm writing you anyway hoping your mother will read this to you when you call home. First off, I am not coming to court to testify on you. They may have been trying to locate me and threaten to take my baby away from me if I didn't testify against you. That's right Face...when you went in I found out that I was pregnant. We have a beautiful son together who I named Fayzon. He's yours Face! Also I wanted to point out that I feel as if we both played a role in how things turned out. You've cheated, and so have I. I was wrong for calling the police on you while you were sleep, but I didn't know you had a gun on you. I apologize and I still and always will love you...even after almost taking my life. I forgive you. Our love is a toxic love, but I wouldn't trade you for nothing or nobody! I feel like the case against you is weak, and you'll be home soon. When you do come home please call me...your son needs you! 772-555-4292.

KoKo

Face took a lighter from his pocket and lit the letter on fire. He watched it burn, then dropped it in his mother's toilet and flushed it.

"What was that?" Pandora asked.

Face exhaled deeply. "A letter from KoKo."

Chapter 4
Devil's Pie

When Face stepped out of his mother's house, he spotted Moses and his sister Sierra sitting up under a gazebo, smoking and drinking. Even though the letter from KoKo had him in a state of ambivalence, he masked it and smiled while approaching the crowd.

"Face boy, you got nine lives! Wass hadnin, my nigga?" Moses greeted, standing to dap Face up.

"Wass poppin'?" Face retorted.

"Same shit, gettin' to the money. Matter fact, shid…let me holla ar'cha right quick," Moses pronounced, walking off with Face following.

"Damn, he just came home! Let'em vibe wit' family. You can talk bidness later!" Sierra asserted, scrunching up her face.

"Chill out wit' all that!" Moses retorted seriously.

Sierra continued to frown but remained quiet. Moses stopped in the middle of the driveway, leaned on his Dodge Magnum, and handed Face the joint that he was smoking.

"Listen homie, I'm glad to see you back out here! I'on know how you came from up under that, but that's the past. We finna get this money in the present."

"Hold up partna," Face interjected smoothly, putting the back of his hand on Moses' chest.

"Look me up on Pacer. Before we do bidness, check my paperwork out. Homie, I'm lightweight tired of hearing that shit," Face voiced calmly, then hit the blunt.

"Nawl, it ain't nothin' like that family. I know you solid! I just meant that God was wit'chu. I'll neva come at'chu like that, you trippin' my nigga," Moses corrected.

"I hear you. Wassup though?" Face questioned, passing the blunt back to Moses.

"I got twenty P's for you. Just give me a stack apiece," Moses told'em.

"What it is?"

"Runts! Straight pressure," Moses boasted, flicking the roach on the pavement.

"I call that," Face accepted.

"Aight, I got'em in the garage. Listen, I wanna ask you somethin' though."

Face looked Moses in his eyes.

"Wassup?" Face implored, folding his arms across his chest.

"You still fuckin' wit' KoKo?"

"Come on, man. Hell fuck nawl!"

"Okay," Moses retorted, shaking his head in approval. "Fam, from me to you...you a real solid nigga. Everybody ain't meant to be around you. Everybody don't deserve yo energy. In life, it's levels. It's levels to life and sometimes you gotta leave a muthafucka at that low level and transcend to that level you know you 'pose to be vibrating on. All that givin' bitches a chance who you know don't deserve it is a dubb. That shit is a waste of time, and I'm sho' I'm pullin' yo coat on some shit that you already know."

Face listened assiduously, feeling every word that Moses was dropping.

"I'm only tellin' you this kuz I fuck wit'cha fam."

"Shit deep," Face added.

"Yea, I done been there, fam. A bitch can have the most flamin' mouth and pussy in the world...but when the shit be toxic, it ain't nothin' but a slice of the Devil's pie, homie," Moses voiced.

Listening to Moses talk caused Face to have flashes of all the deadly and toxic moments he had with KoKo. Realizing how foolish he'd been making himself look, he felt as if he was having a sucka attack. Face quickly composed himself and got down to bidness.

"I feel you bra. I'm focus, nah let's get to it," Face stated.

***

Later on that night, around 8:35 p.m., Face said his goodbyes and told B3 that it was time to hit it. Once to his car, World called out to Face and made his way towards him.

"Bra, wassup? Let's hit the club," World proposed, hyped up.

Face pondered the idea for a moment.

"Ion know bra. I really wanted to just lay back in my shit and relax...like I'm really free, my nigga. A nigga want a lil time to his self," Face explained.

"Maaan! Fuck you wanna be in the house for, after bein' lockdown for over a year? You can get some alone time when you leave the club. Shid, if I was you, I'll be tryin' to fuck somethin'," World added.

Face looked at B3.

"What'chu wanna do, B3?"

"Shid, I'm wit' you mane."

"Maan! Everything on me!" World pronounced, going in his pocket and handing Face a stack. "Where you stayin' at?"

"I got my spot back on 25th at the Carter," Face informed.

"Aight bet. I'ma pull up round 11:30. Me and TJ," World asserted before spinning off.

Face and B3 hopped in the K5 and got in the wind.

"So, wassup 3?"

"How you mean, mane?" B3 implored.

"You gettin' money?"

"I do a lil somethin'. Sometimes, I go cut grass wit' my folks, or I might do a lil roofing, mane. Why, wassup? You need a job, mane?"

Face laughed at B3's gesture.

"Nawl, homie. I ain't workin' for no kraka. I asked you that to see if you wanna get some money. I'on trust nobody, my nigga, and you been rockin' out wit' me," Face voiced.

"Mane, hell yeah I want some money, mane. What we talkin' mane?" B3 asked as Face pulled on the side of the road in front of B3's girl public housing apartment. Face popped the trunk.

"Look homie. Grab one of them duffel bags out my trunk. It's ten cans in there. Give me two bands apiece, homie," Face proclaimed, watching his surroundings.

"What's in the cans, mane?"

"Ten pounds of Runts. Straight pressure, homie," Face pronounced, grabbing his strap and placing it on his lap.

He noted the crowd of niggaz down the street in KoKo's mother yard looking in their direction.

"I got'cha, mane. I appreciate that, mane," B3 said, dapping Face up and pulling the FN from his britches to hand back to him.

"Nah, homie, that's you nah. Make sho' you brang it wit'chu when we hit the club."

"Fasho, mane! I'll be ready when you pull up, mane," B3 assured, stepping out of the whip.

He grabbed a duffel then headed inside. Face pulled off, creeping behind five percent tint. When he slid past KoKo's mother house, G-man and his homies were outside. Some were carelessly slipping while others were on point clutching their weapons. Face smiled behind the tint as he crept on by.

"I'ma get'chu, tough ass nigga," Face mumbled to himself.

Chapter 5
All Love

The club was so packed that Face and B3 had to park at the Amaco across the street, with World and TJ behind them. Everybody tucked their pistols and stepped out. World approached Face with a velvet bag and handed it to him.

"This all ya jewelz, nigga. I added a lil' somethin' too, nothin' major," World proclaimed, smiling, happy to be out with his brother.

Face opened the bag and put the statement pieces on one by one. He put the Cubans on his neck and wrist but paused when he grabbed the Rolex from the bag.

"Yeah, that's from me, nigga. Lil' plain Jane, Oyster Perpetual," World boasted.

"Bet that up, fam," said Face, dapping and hugging his brother's neck.

"You shinin' nah, mane," B3 added.

"Wass poppin', TJ? You good?" Face implored.

"Yeah, big homie, I'm Gucci. Let's be out though," TJ suggested.

The four-pack moved in synch, crossing the highway, watching all angles. When they made it in front of the Elk's Lounge, the line was a little meaty.

"Man, this line too long, my nigga. Hand me two hundred," Face told World when he spotted Big Rude, who was the bouncer.

Big Rude lived across the street from Face's mother's house. TJ pulled out a hunid, and World pulled out another one.

"Come on, follow me," Face stated, walking to the front of the line.

"Aye Rude! Wassup, my nigga?" Face greeted.

Rude did a double take then smiled.

"Face, boy, what up?" Rude spoke back, grabbing Face's hand and pulling him close for a hug.

Face quickly whispered in Rude's ear.

"I got fo' hunid for fo' of us."

"Shid, I got'cha," Rude assured.

Face slipped him the billz, then nodded his head at his crew to follow. All of them slipped inside without being searched.

***

That booty sit up / like two bunk beds
Oh, she thick-thick / She eat her cornbread
The sounds of Bossman DLow permeated the atmosphere, provoking the majority of the women to twerk vehemently while reciting every word.

"Man, I hate this stupid-ass song!" Face yelled at World.

"Nigga, you sleep! Bossman DLow be cookin'!" World defended as they approached the bar.

"Four cups of Don Julio!" World ordered. "Straight!" he added.

The bartender, who resembled Keyshia Cole, quickly made the drinks, cutting her eye at Face the entire time.

"That'll be forty-eight dollars even!"

World paid the tab, but Face put a fifty-dollar bill on the bar for a tip.

"Thank you," she asserted, smiling.

Face shook his head up and down. The bartender motioned for Face to come closer.

"Wassup," Face implored.

"Hand me yo' phone," she demanded.

Face handed her the phone and watched her log her name in.

"I'm Kayla. Call me, anytime," she advised, smiling before leaving to serve another customer.

The four-pack mobbed off and found a spot in the cut.

"Nigga, you pulled one then," World admitted.

"Hell yeah, mane, she bad," B3 added.

TJ just smiled and nodded his head to the music. Moments later, they all sparked their blunts in tandem.

"Boy, them hoes is in here!" World yelled excitedly, taking his phone out to go live. "Yeah, nigga! My brother back out'chere on you bitch-ass niggas! We catchin' bodies like cheerleaders and beatin' them shits like dope in a beaker! Get'cha hat count up! Big Bully Gang or no hang! Bddaaatt!" World boasted, holding his phone up with Face, B3, and TJ behind him.

"Bddaaatt!" Face yelled, throwing up Big B's and blowing smoke in the camera.

A slew of people joined World's live with remarks dedicated to Face's freedom.

"Bra, look at this shit! You lit!"

When Face glanced at World's phone, he seen a comment that dampened his mood a lil' bit. It was a comment from KoKo saying *welcome home and call me.* Face quickly waved his hand in dismissal.

"Get that shit out my face, bra!" Face stated, taking a sip from his cup and a toke from his blunt afterwards.

"Don't let that hoe kill yo' vibe! You free, big brah!"

Face nodded his head in agreement.

"Heey, Face!" a slim-thick red beauty sang, stopping in front of Face.

"Lexus?" Face implored.

Lexus shook her head up and down, smiling.

"Yep! It's good to see you. How you been?" Lexus asked, closing the space between them.

Face quickly put an arm around her, gripping her pillow-soft ass cheek.

"I been me, you know. It's good to run into you, too," he retorted.

"Ummm. I'm wit'chu tonight?" Lexus questioned, grabbing a handful of Face's dick.

Knowing how Lexus got down, Face was aroused instantly.

"Yeah, you wit' me. Don't go nowhere. Matter of fact, here," Face reached in his pocket and handed Lexus some money. "Go get'chu a drink and come right back," he ordered.

"Okay, daddy," Lexus retorted seductively before strutting off in a Burberry bodysuit and Christian Louboutin heels.

"Boy, I see you, mane! Lexus done got thick, mane!" B3 asserted.

"Yeah, she lookin' like somethin'," Face added, when a tall nigga approached with a crew behind him. TJ, who was quiet most of the night, quickly snatched his FNH .40 from his Purple Brand pants, with World and B3 following suit.

"Da fuck is up, nigga?" TJ barked warily.

"Wass poppin'?" World added.

Face inhaled and exhaled sharply, blowing smoke while posting behind his niggaz, smiling.

"Oh, dey got da blix in!" C-Rock intoned questionably.

"What it is, what it ain't?" Face interjected, while Lexus approached from the side.

Face wrapped his arm around her, bringing her close.

"Well, first off, it ain't no smoke, so you can call ya shooters off. I just came over here to show love, my nigga," C-Rock explained, reaching his hand out for Face to embrace, but World and TJ pushed him back aggressively.

"Back da fuck up, nigga!" World yelled, pointing his pistol at C-Rock, while TJ and B3 waved theirs back and forth at C-Rock's homies.

A crowd of people scattered in fear. Face took his arm from around Lexus and stepped in front of his homies. He then motioned for them to put their guns down. Facing C-Rock, Face held his hand out for C-Rock to embrace.

"It's all love, homie! You welcome on this side of town anytime, my nigga," Face enunciated.

C-Rock shook Face's hand and shook his head in understanding. C-Rock then walked off with his lil' homies muggin' Face and his niggaz.

"Who da fuck was that nigga?" World questioned, tucking his pistol.

"I did time wit' em. He from 13th Street," Face informed.

"Y'all good?" World questioned.

"Yeah, we aight. We got on some nigga top together when we was up the road."

"That's that nigga from earlier, mane!" B3 pointed out.

"Yeah," Face assured.

"Earlier?" World questioned.

"It ain't nothin'," Face assured.

"You okay, daddy?" Lexus asked, wrapping her arms around Face.

"Yeah. You ready to slide?" Face asked, having seen enough excitement for the night.

"Aye, I'm out! I'm finna slide," Face told his niggaz.

"Man, we jist got here! I'ma hang out," World stated.

"I'ma stay here wit' deez boys, mane," B3 added.

"Aight," Face retorted, dapping B3 and TJ up.

He then peaced World up before leaving.

"Eastside," World yelled.

"All the time," Face replied, leaving the club with Lexus.

Chapter 6
Fuck Back

The sound of Lexus' saturated pussy echoed throughout Face's apartment as he stroked her to an eloquent rhythm. For every stroke he delivered, pussy juice cascaded from her womb profusely.

"Oooowww, you got this pussy so fuckin' wet, daddy! Ssss...aah...sssshit! Ssss...yesss, daddy, haaaah!" Lexus cried, holding both of her legs in the air herself while watching Face slip in and out of her.

"Sssss...ffffuck!" Face yelled, snatching out of her wet, warm, vice grip-like pussy.

He beat her clit with the head of his dick, then maneuvered it on her clit from side to side, coating it with pre-cum. This method was a cheat code to keep him from cumming prematurely.

"Put that dick back in me, please!" Lexus cried while her pussy throbbed. Face could actually see her womb opening and closing with anticipation.

"Damn," Face mumbled, slipping back into Lexus' goodness for four strokes before snatching out again and rubbing his dick on her clit.

"Fffffuck! Stop playin' wit' me! Just fuck me, please!" Lexus moaned.

"Shut the fuck up!" Face barked, grabbing her left leg and moving it to her right, causing her petite, thick frame to flip over.

"Umm hmm!" Lexus sang, placing her head down, ass up with an impeccable deep arch in her back.

Her pussy sat beautifully and beefy from the back like ripe fruit. Face slapped her ass cheek a few times, then slipped in her wetness from behind.

"Ffffuck! This pussy, butter!" Face moaned, stroking her slow, long, and deep.

Without warning, Lexus turned her head to the side and started to throw her pussy back rapidly, watching Face out of her peripheral.

"Sssshit! That's it, throw that shit back!" Face motivated.

"Mmmhmmm! Ssss, yeah! I fuck back! This pussy fucks back, daddy!"

"Ssshit, yeah! Get this dick!"

Smack! Face slapped Lexus' ass aggressively, biting his bottom lip.

"Ooowee! Sss...ffffuck! You feel that pussy? Huh? Sss...answer me nigga! You feel this pussy grippin'?" Lexus moaned through clenched teeth, throwing her pussy back while cumming all over Face's dick.

He could feel her nectar drippin' from his dick.

"Shut the fuck up, bitch!" Face yelled, pinning the small of her back to the mattress and fucking her violently.

Lexus buried her face in the pillow and took all that Face produced.

"Yeah! Talk that shit to the fuckin' pillow, bitch! Huh? Huh? I don't fuckin' hear you!" Face barked, cumming powerfully inside of Lexus' sodden pussy.

She felt Face growing inches longer inside her and lost her mind.

"Aaaaaaaahh...Ole God! Ffffuck, daddy, I'm fuckin' cumming on that dick, baby!" Lexus screamed, looking back at Face while gripping the pillow.

"Ummmm hmmmm!" Face moaned, releasing all that he had inside of her.

"Fffuck," they moaned in unison as Face stroked her slow.

Lexus leaned forward, causing Face to slip out of her, turned around, and cleaned Face's dick with her mouth. She knew how sensitive the head of his dick was after cumming, so she made it her business to suck on it perpetually.

"Ffffuck!" Face cried, prying her mouth from his dick. "That's enough! Fuck! What'chu tryin' to do?"

"I want'chu, Face," Lexus admitted.

"What'chu mean?" Face implored bleakly. "You just had me."

"No, I want'chu to myself," she enunciated.

"You trippin', Lex. Look, we can link up, but I ain't on that relationship shit right nah. I done been through too much," Face explained, feeling emotionally depleted.

Lexus exhaled deeply, brimming with emotion.

"I understand. I'll settle for a piece of you rather than have none."

"Fasho," Face pronounced, gazing at the ceiling with one hand behind his head.

"Face, can I tell you something?" Lexus asked in a molly tone.

"Wassup?"

"I never liked the way KoKo treated you. I always felt like you deserved better," she voiced, rubbing Face's chest tenderly.

"Yeah. It took a minute, but I know that nah," Face admitted.

"Do you remember the day she came in my apartment and told you that Irvin was outside, and he was touching on her? She said he just popped up, remember?"

"Yeah, I know you know, I killed that nigga," Face stated, staring deep into her enchanting hazel pupils.

"I know, but the thing is, Face, KoKo lied to you. I was right there when she called him and told him to come see her. She so trifling that she really set him up for cheating on her when they were together. On top of that, she had heard how you got down and wanted to see it up close and personal."

Face took in everything that Lexus dropped. After replaying the episode with Irvin, it all made sense. He exhaled, seething.

"After everything I been through wit' that hoe, that shit don't even surprise me. I appreciate'chu though," Face asserted, kissing Lexus on her forehead.

"No problem. If I can be honest wit'chu, Face... I wish you would've killed her," Lexus expressed, laying her head on Face's chest.

Face exhaled deeply while running his hands through her natural, sandy-colored hair.

"Me too," Face retorted.

Chapter 7
Murda Courtesy

Face was awakened the next evening by the sound of his phone blowing up. He squirmed and stretched before becoming fully conscious. Lexus was already awake watching him while he slept. She was now placing kisses on his chest.

"Ummmm, good morning, ma," Face greeted, grabbing her by her throat and kissing her on the forehead.

"Mornin', daddy," she retorted, placing a trail of wet kisses down his chest.

Face looked at his phone and saw that B3 had called numerous times and a number he didn't recognize. He called B3 back while Lexus began to suck his dick slow and passionately.

"Wassup, mane?"

"Yo," Face retorted, biting his bottom lip.

"Say mane, I done moved six of them cans, mane! Shit groovin' over this way here, mane!" B3 stated proudly.

"Sssshit! Aight, nigga! Wat'chu want, a hug?" Face clowned through clenched teeth.

"Aye mane! I know you ain't gettin' topped off while on the phone wit' me, mane!"

"You are correct on your assumption, nigga! Nigga, hit my line when you done!"

"Yeah, mane. Oh, and I forgot to tell you mane! I gave—!"

Click! Face hung up on B3 and grabbed the back of Lexus' head while she bobbed up and down proficiently until she made him cum in her mouth. Lexus swallowed everything eagerly.

"Look, it's brand-new toothbrushes in there, soap, rags, and towels," Face offered.

Lexus chuckled.

"Thank you, daddy, but I'm finna go home and get all that right. You gone pull up on me later?" Lexus implored with puppy eyes.

"I'll do what I can," Face said, his phone ringing moments later.

"Who the fuck is this?" Face snapped, not recognizing the number.

"Heeeyyy, daddy! Oooo, I missed you so much!"

Face's flesh started to crawl at the sound of the caller's voice.

"How the fuck you get my number?" Face questioned, seething as his breath quickened and his pressure began to rise.

"B3 gave it to me! Why? You don't want me to have it?" KoKo asked, fake surprised.

"Bitch, don't neva hit my line again, hoe! You dead to me!"

"Wait! Face, please! Please don't hang up!" KoKo begged.

Click! Face hung up in her face, then reached for a pre-rolled blunt of strawberry Runts and sparked it.

"That was KoKo, huh?" Lexus asked.

Face nodded his head yes while blowing smoke from his nose. He hated KoKo, but the sound of her voice stirred something inside him. Face was conflicted. His phone rang again, but this time Lexus snatched it and answered. Face didn't protest.

"Umm, KoKo, you need to stop calling this phone! You done took this man through all kind of toxic shit that he didn't deserve! You had a good man, but you fucked that up!

Move on! It's over, KoKo!" Lexus snapped, not having one gangsta bone in her body.

"Lexus? Wait, hold up! What the fuck you doin' round my nigga?" KoKo snapped.

"KoKo, you delulu! Face is not yo man!" Lexus enunciated, her tone denoting anger.

"So, what'chu sayin', hoe? He suppose to be yo nigga nah?"

"KoKo, I can't tell you what this is, but I can tell you what it ain't! And it damn sho' ain't you! Nah, stop callin' this phone!"

Click! Lexus hung up on KoKo, quivering with excitement.

"You aight?" Face asked, observing her body language.

He knew that when KoKo caught Lexus in traffic it was sure to be a violent collision.

"Yeah, I'm just agitated with her insolence," she stated, grabbing the blunt from Face's fingers and taking a toke.

"You do know she gone want smoke behind that, right?"

"I'm not afraid of KoKo. She can probably beat my ass, but I'm not afraid of her. Besides, you worth it, daddy," she proclaimed, blowing smoke from her nose.

"I hear you, just be careful," Face warned.

***

Proficient killaz / type of niggaz I was raised wit' /

You don't like me / load up, pull up / give me to the pavement /

If I survive da spank / yo people gone find out who you played wit' /

Boy, you gettin' slayed / death ensured like AIDS Vic /

How you droppin' all dis murda music / but ain't slayed shit /

Amusin' / everythang around you dyin' in amazement /

Wallalhi / did slime, um goin' to my grave wit' /

I'on wit' all dhat lookin' over my shoulder / dhat's enslavement /

Um Bloody ana / the dirt that I dot it out was muddy ana /

He don't like me / my lil parna stepped on his lil buddy ana…

The sounds of Big Khufu galvanized the animalistic side of Face and B3's being while they circulated the same four blocks in a murder bucket. Face pulled on a blunt white cap, then passed it to B3 who was driving.

"Say mane, let me eat wit'chu, mane," B3 pleaded, taking a toke from the blunt afterwards.

"Nawl, you doin' what I need you to do. I got it," Face explained, watching everything outside the car while they combed the streets.

"You wit' the bullshit, mane. It's after three in the mornin' anyway, mane, ain't nobody out hurr, mane," B3 pronounced, speaking too soon.

When they turned down Twentieth Street, Face spotted who he was looking for. He reached in the back seat and grabbed a blonde thirty-inch wig and pulled it over his deep waves.

"Pull over, up there field they be trappin' in," Face ordered, gripping his FN Five-Seven and letting his window down.

He turned down the music and called from the passenger seat.

"Come here, lil daddy!" Face yelled seductively as if he were a woman.

"Who that?" Ant inquired, dipped in all black with a red bandanna around his neck.

Ant carelessly made his way toward the passenger window, enticed by the blonde wig.

"Ooooww, I got'em," Face mumbled to himself.

He quickly upped his pistol and fired rapidly.

Boc! Boc! Boc! Bullets penetrated the left side of Ant's chest, spinning him around. Out of pure instinct, Ant turned and ran for his life, but Face was already hopping out of the whip after him.

"Come here! Where you goin', lil daddy?" Face clowned, planting four more shots in his back, dropping him portentously.

Ant fell face first, then turned over on his back to face his killer. Ant was a piece of shit without a doubt, but what everybody knew was... he was gangsta.

"Wass poppin', Blood?" Face inquired as he stood over his man.

Boc! Boc! Boc! Blood oozed out with every intake of breath, staining his clothes a dark maroon. He planted four more in his chest, then trotted back to the murder bucket and hopped in with B3, who pulled off smoothly.

"You hit the nigga in the head, mane?" B3 questioned.

"Nawl, I made sho' his people can view him with his casket open. You know, a lil murda courtesy," Face disclosed impassively.

B3 glanced at Face, then back at the road.

"Say mane, how many hats you got?" B3 asked curiously, secretly admiring Face's gangsta.

Face lit a spliff, took a deep pull, and exhaled slowly before replying.

"To be honest wit'chu, fam, I'on even count no more. But I can tell you this—every time you take a soul, a part of yours leave wit' it too. That's the part they don't tell you," Face explained to B3, knowing that he was craving for a body.

B3 pondered Face's words, then shook his head in understanding.

Chapter 8
They Fakin'

The next day, a little after noon, Face pulled on the side of the brownstone and hopped out with a brown paper bag and his pistol glued to his side. When Face ascended the second half of the stairs, Shooter and Lil Fif God stopped him.

"Whoa, homie! Wass poppin'?" Lil Fif God implored.

"Niggaz like us!" Face retorted.

"I hear you, but what'chu doin' here? You gotta appointment wit' the Queen?" Lil Fif God asked while Shooter held his pistol by his side.

"Hold up, my nigga! First off, I'm Damu! So, you lil niggaz either salute me, or shoot me!" Face stated, seething.

In that moment, the door to the apartment opened.

"Salute 'em and let 'em up!" Assata demanded.

Face looked up at Assata and admired her beauty. He then smirked at her drops.

"We gotta pat him down, Queen," Lil Fif God asserted.

"What did I say?" Assata barked.

Shooter and Lil Fif God peaced Face up, then let him by.

"Wass poppin', Queen?" Face greeted, bumping B's with Assata.

"Us, neva them," she retorted, nodding her head for him to come inside.

Face silently admired her designer décor.

"You wanna have a seat?" she offered, taking one herself.

"No, thank you," Face decided, handing her the brown bag.

"What this is?"

"Twenty."

Assata didn't even look in the bag; she just sat it on a red-stained table then sparked a blunt.

"I viewed that episode on Facebook. They said he was fighting for his life but died on his way to surgery. Nice demo, I'm impressed," Assata admitted.

"That's light work. Anytime, Bloody, just holla dinner time," Face asserted.

Assata had declared Ant a plate for starting a Blood set without sanction. Face took the plate readily, not liking Ant anyway. Assata lapsed into a simmering silence, observing Face's panache while ponderous moments ticked by. She inhaled deeply, then exhaled slowly.

"What rims you got?" Assata inquired, crossing her legs seductively.

"I'ma Sweeper," Face informed, referring to his stain or status.

"Hmmm." She sighed, nodding her head in approval of his rank as a five-star General.

Face's phone rang, breaking the gaze between the two. It was a number he didn't recognize, so he didn't answer in case it was KoKo.

"I want the same number for them other twenty cans," Assata declared.

"What other twenty?"

"The ones that Shooter put in yo' back seat."

Face displayed an expression of incredulity.

"They already in ya whip, homie. I'ma bark at 'chu later," she proclaimed, blowing smoke from her nose.

"Aight then, two-twelve Damu," Face replied, placing five fingers and his palm against his heart.

"Wooooop!" Assata responded before Face left her apartment.

***

When Face got in his whip, he looked in the back seat and sure enough the duffle bags were there. He push-started his car then got in traffic. As soon as he reached to turn up the volume to YSW Worldd's *Karma Do It All*, his phone rang again, displaying the same number.

"Yeah, who the fuck is this?" he snapped.

"Damn, kuz! Calm down, this me, Chere!"

Chere was Face's cousin who was a booster of clothes and liquor.

"Oh, wass poppin', family? How you livin'?" Face inquired.

"I'm good! You know I got my own boutique in Jensen Beach."

"Nawl? Shid…that's wassup! I'ma pull up and fuck wit'chu," Face promised.

"That's kinda why I called you. I want'chu to pull up, fame."

"What'chu need me to handle somethin'?"

"Nawl, kuz! Even if I did, I wouldn't call you. Kuz, you just got out," Chere proclaimed.

"I'on give no fucks bout that! Bout'chu, I'm comin'!"

"I know, kuz! Can you just pull up on me, please?" begged Chere.

"Yeah, wea you at? The jects?"

"I'on live there no mo'. I just handle bidness there sometimes, but yeah I'm in the jects."

"I'm on my way. But answer me this—how you get my number?" Face wanted to know.

"Sierra gave it to me! Damn, kuz, you don't want me wit' the number?"

"Yeah, you good. I'm in ya chest in a minute!"

Click! Face hung up as he pulled in front of B3's spot and blew the horn. Moments later, B3 stepped out and made his way towards Face's whip and got into the passenger's seat.

"Wassup, mane?" B3 asked, elated to see Face.

"Same shit, different toilet. Wass poppin' wit'chu?" Face implored, dapping B3 up.

"Everything good, mane! I'm just waitin' on you, mane. My phone ringin' off the hook, mane."

Face shook his head up and down.

"I hear you. Don't trip, I got'chu."

"Oh yeah, mane. I was tryin' to tell you the other day, mane, that I gave KoKo yo number, mane," B3 confessed.

Face looked at B3 with an expression of disappointment, shaking his head from side to side.

"Why the fuck would you do that?"

"I'on know, mane. I just feel like a conversation needs to take place, mane."

"You trippin'!" Face snapped.

"Also, mane, KoKo brother asked me who drivin' this car, mane. I told 'em my people from Mississippi," B3 proclaimed.

"Oh yeah?" Face implored, looking in his rearview, spotting a Jeep Cherokee approaching with an arm hanging from the passenger's window.

"Get right, shit behind us look creep," Face warned, gripping his pistol.

Face seen the arm disappear in the window and reappear holding a weapon.

Boc! Boc! Boc! Boc! Four shots rang out, all hitting Face's window, who had ducked his head ahead of time. When the Jeep passed by, Face opened his door, stood in his door frame, and returned fire. B3 followed suit, letting off a barrage of fire.

"Grab the duffels out of the back seat!" Face ordered B3.

B3 tucked his pistol and did as he was told.

"I want twenty for 'em. I'ma hit'cha line later, homie," Face enunciated, pulling off soon after B3 grabbed the bags.

"Who the fuck was that?" he thought to himself. "Whoever it was, fakin'!" he continued to ponder while he headed to Chere's apartment.

As soon as Face pulled into Chere's driveway, his phone rang.

"Wassup?" he answered.

"Face, you okay?" Lexus asked.

"Yeah, I'm good, ma," he assured.

"I was looking out my window when I seen them shooting at 'chu! Oh my God! My heart is beating so fast right now!"

"Yeah, some niggaz tried it, but they was fakin'. I appreciate 'chu checkin' on me, that's wassup."

"No problem. Face, I gotta tell you something," Lexus asserted.

"I'm listening," Face told her.

"Come see me tonight. It's real important, Face," she stated seriously.

"I'ma be there, you hear me?" Face assured.

"Okay."

Click!

Chapter 9
Fatherly Love

When Face stepped out of his car Chere was standing outside of his door waiting. She quickly hugged and kissed him on the cheek. "Kuz, you aight?" Chere questioned, looking at the holes in his window.

"Yeah, bitch ass niggaz drove by hittin' at my shit. They was supposed to hop out and give it to me, but they was amateurs," Face clowned, chuckling.

"Boy, that ain't funny, wit'cha crazy ass! Come on inside. I wanna sho' you somethin'," Chere asserted, pulling Face by the hand.

Entering the apartment, Face noted bottles of liquor everywhere. "What'chu wanted to sho' me, fam?" Face questioned.

"Have a drink wit' me first, kuz," Chere suggested.

"Yeah, po' up."

"What'chu wanna drink?"

"Grab that Remy! You know that's all I drank," Face announced, having a seat in one of Chere's butter-soft, peanut butter leather sofas.

Chere poured herself a shot then handed Face the whole bottle. "Here, this yo bottle. Make a toast, fam," Chere declared, clinging her shot glass against his bottle. "To you being free," she announced. "Salute!" Chere downed her shot while Face took a healthy swig from the bottle.

After several more shots, Face was feeling a little tipsy. "Damn, fam, what'chu wanted to sho me?" Face asked curiously.

"Aight, look. Don't be mad at me," Chere pleaded, standing up and heading to her bedroom door that was only a few steps away from the couch where Face was seated.

"Fuck you got goin' on?" Face inquired.

When Chere opened her door, KoKo came prancing out looking like a snack in a Saint Laurent mini dress and Red Bottom heels.

"Da fuck is this?" Face snapped, snatching his pistol from his joggers.

"Kuz, just calm down," Chere said lifting her hands in the air.

"You tryna set me up?" Face barked, standing to his feet.

Chere looked at Face in disappointment. "Come on, kuz, you know me better than that. Stop playin' wit' me. You know I fuck with KoKo, and from what I'm hearing, you at least owe her a conversation. If you don't like what she gotta say, that's fine too, but at least hear her out," Chere negotiated.

"Please just let me get this off my chest," KoKo added.

Face exhaled deeply while taking a seat.

"Look, I'll be back in a lil' while, fam. Please don't kill her in my house, if that's what'chu thinkin'," Chere asserted, making her way to the front door.

"Really, Chere?" KoKo implored.

"I'm just sayin'," Chere retorted, locking the door behind her.

KoKo locked eyes with Face, perceiving the emotional trauma behind them. She could feel the resentment vibrating from his magnetic aura. Taking a seat across from him, she crossed her legs and exhaled deeply. "Look, first off, thank you for stayin'. Forreal, you could just get up and leave, but'chu stayed to hear me out…thank you. Okay, secondly, it's somethin' I never told you about me. When I was 14 years old, I talked to my father for the first time over the phone. He told me he wanted to spend time with his daughter and agreed to pick me up that weekend. When he picked me up, I was so fuckin' happy to see him. You know every little girl loves and needs that fatherly love. We was supposed to go to the movies, but he told me he needed to stop by his room to take a shower. Thinkin' nothin' of it, I go in and watch TV while he takes his shower. Instead of getting dressed in the bathroom, he comes out the shower naked and forced himself on me.

"When I started crying and askin' him, 'Daddy why you doin' this to me?' he grabbed a pillow and placed it over my head to muffle my cries. Do you know this man had the nerve to still take me to the movies? I had to sit through the whole movie after being raped, and couldn't tell nobody 'cause I was afraid," KoKo explained, her voice cracking as tears fell from her eyes.

Face felt some type of way about her father raping her but masked his feelings.

"My father is a big nigga, so I was afraid to say somethin'. Before he dropped me off to my mama's, he told me that what we did was a little secret. As soon as I got in the house, I cried to my mama and told her what happened. It crushed me to hear her say that it was my fault for being fast, and that I better not say nothin' to nobody," KoKo enunciated, wiping the tears from her face. "I had to call my grandma and tell her what happened. She came to my mama house with the police. My so-called father is in prison right now, and I guess you know my mama put me out. I had to stay wit' my grandma. That shit wit' my father fucked my mind up. I started lookin' for fatherly love in older men that I was fuckin' wit' in the streets. I neva found it. All they did was use me and put me on pills and coke. I been through a lot of shit, Face, which is why I treat niggaz how I treat 'em.

"I'm so afraid of being hurt that I rush to be the victimizer rather than the victim, but on God, you the only nigga I ever gave my heart to. I love you, nigga! Even after trying to kill me, I love you, and I'm sorry I called the police on you.

When I came home, I seen you in the bed. I panicked because I had a nigga wit' me. I would've never called them if I knew you had a gun on you. Please, Face, I promise on our son, I'll neva play police games wit'chu again." KoKo proclaimed.

"Where he at?" Face inquired, saying something for the first time.

"My sister got'em while I'm here," KoKo retorted, standing, making her way over to Face and kneeling before him.

Face gazed at her, his expression granite while she slipped his semi-hard dick from his Palm Angles.

"I missed you, daddy," KoKo confessed, swallowing him whole until he grew his full length and caused her to gag. "Mmmmmmhmmm!" KoKo moaned as she sucked and slurped with sufficient passion while Face remained silent, feeling like a sucka for even allowing her to touch him.

A part of him still loved her through the bullshit, but he wasn't really feeling her at the moment. "Hold up," Face interjected, grabbing her by her weave and pulling her mouth away from his dick.

"Wass wrong, daddy?" KoKo asked confused.

"Let's go in Chere room," he suggested, standing with his dick still swinging.

Without protest KoKo got up and headed to the room. Once in the room, Face made her kneel in front of the bed. He grabbed the back of her head, then grabbed his dick to spank both sides of her face.

"Mmmmhmmm!" she moaned.

Face spanked her lips then rubbed the head of his dick back and forth, spreading precum all over them. KoKo quickly licked her lips and swallowed.

"Open yo mouth," he demanded, and she obeyed. "Eat that dick up!"

With that command, KoKo activated into animalistic mode, sucking with purpose.

Face's toes curled in his Vapor Maxes. "Ssss...fffffuck!" Face moaned, snatching out of her mouth and busting all over KoKo's face.

"Oooow, it's so warm, daddy," she announced.

"Get up! Get in the bed and boot over," Face ordered.

"Mmmmhm, get this pussy," KoKo stated, hiking her dress up and climbing in the bed.

"Put an arch in that shit, and put'cha face in the pillow."

"Ummm!" she added, doing as she was told. Moments ticked by with no penetration. "Come on, daddy," KoKo cried, finally looking behind her only to find Face gone. "Bae! Daddy!" she called out, climbing out of the bed. When she looked in the living room, Face was nowhere in sight. She looked out the door and noted that Face's car was gone.

Chapter 10
Where My Son At?

KoKo had been calling Face's phone all day, only to get sent to voicemail. It was now close to 10:30 p.m., and she was still calling.

"Just pick up and tell her it's over, mane," B3 advised, smoking a blunt.

"Nawl, I gotta let her think it's still some type of chance so she won't call them krakaz," Face pronounced, smoking a blunt of his own.

"I already told her that it was over, and she need to stop calling his phone," Lexus added, then took a toke from her Newport.

"Say what, mane? Ain't no way in hell you told KoKo no shit like that, mane."

"And did," Lexus confirmed, rubbing her hand across Face's lap.

"She ain't come to see you yet?" B3 inquired, scrunching up his face.

"No," Lexus retorted, still fondling Face's genitals.

"You gotta be careful, mane."

"Ummhmm, whatever," Lexus mumbled.

Face's phone rang again, but this time he answered.

"Wass poppin', brodi?" Face answered.

"Niggaz like us!" World proclaimed.

"Whoop!" Face retorted.

"Damn, bra, you don't fuck wit' a nigga? Been a few dayz, yeen hit a nigga line or nothin'! What'chu hidin' from somethin'?" World clowned.

"Imagine that. I ain't gone hold you...I'm on one right nah, but I'ma pull up, prolly tomorrow, fam," Face enunciated.

"You need me?"

"I got it, bra. Appreciate'chu though," Face asserted.

"Respect! Two-twelve Damu," World stated.

"All the time, Bloody," Face replied.

Click!

"Aight, look Lex. You sho' it was them?"

"Face, I'll neva lie to you. I seen them clear as day," Lexus assured.

Face's phone alerted him that he had a text. When he opened it, it was a photo of a baby boy sent from KoKo. Face examined it quickly, then turned the phone off.

"Tighten up, 3," Face ordered, standing and grabbing his new P90 and his ARP.

"Face, please be careful," Lexus pleaded, standing to kiss Face on his cheek.

"This shit light work, don't even trip," Face asserted, heading towards the back door with B3 behind him.

They both were in all-black turtlenecks, black Dickies, and black Air Maxes. Before leaving out the door, Face cut the kitchen lights, then wrapped a blue bandana round his face while B3 did the same. Creeping on the back porch, Suga Mama could be seen standing over the stove cooking what smelt like fried chicken. The duo slipped by unnoticed and rounded the back of Suga Mama's adjacent apartment, gripping their weapons.

The backside of the apartment was clear, but when they rounded the side of the apartment, two males could be seen stepping out of a Genesis. Face got low and crept up behind a bush that sat on the side of the apartment, with B3 behind him. When the two men made their way to the porch, Face crept swiftly and rounded the front of Suga Mama's apartment with B3 right there wit'em. Face lifted his P90 with the flashlight beaming, blinding their prey.

"What's crakin', kuz!"

Boc! Boc! Boc! Boc! Boc! Boc! Boc! Boc!

G-man and the nigga next to him dropped poetically. B3 wet the other two who tried to run away, dropping them and standing over them unloading his whole clip.

"Tighten down," Face yelled, taking off running through a field that was behind the project apartments with B3 behind him.

Face quickly cut through a hole in a fence that lined the back of the apartments and came out on 24th Street in front of the candy lady's house, Ms. Dot. Face jumped in the driver's side of a murder bucket they had parked on 24th Street with B3 hopping in on the passenger side. Dropping the whip in gear, Face disappeared into the night under the Florida moon.

Lexus had informed Face and B3 that it was KoKo's brother G-man and his G.D. homies who had attempted to kill him. She had seen them in the Jeep Cherokee and overheard them talking about it on the porch adjacent to hers. With her newfound emotions towards Face, Lexus found it imperative that she disclose all that she'd heard and seen.

***

The next morning, Face crept past Suga Mama's apartment to examine the pain he'd put in. Her porch and yard were crowded with loved ones who mourned their loss. When Face made it to the corner, he looked back and seen KoKo coming out of Suga Mama's apartment. Face grabbed his phone and called her before pulling off.

"Hello?" KoKo answered, surprisingly in good spirit.

"Wassup? I'm just hittin' you, sending condolences. I'm sorry for ya loss," Face pronounced.

"That's real, Face. I appreciate'chu foreal," KoKo stated.

"No problem."

"I really just need to get away and go clear my head. You feel like coming to get me and taking me somewhere?" she implored.

"Where you tryna go?" Face asked, spinning the block.

"I don't care. Anywhere," KoKo assured, looking up and seeing a black Kia pulling in front of the apartments.

"Aight, I'm here. In this black truck," Face proclaimed.

He had switched vehicles with his sister for a few hours just to see what the streets looked like after his demonstration.

***

Smack...Smack...Smack...Smack! The sounds of Face's flesh smacking against KoKo's echoed throughout the room at Econo Lounge that Face had rented for a few hours. Face had KoKo laid out on her stomach while he stroked her slow, steady, and deep to a delectable rhythm from behind.

"Oooowww, daddy! Sssshit! Pussy skeetin'!" KoKo cried, gripping the pillow as she climaxed all over Face's dick.

Face felt her walls clinching around his girth and came in tandem while kissing her on the back of her neck and the side of her face.

"Whooooo... I feel you, daddy, sssshit!" KoKo cried while Face grinded all that he had left in her.

"Ffffuck, this pussy bitin'," Face retorted as goosebumps crawled up his arms.

He made it his business to fuck KoKo thoroughly to erase all suspicion of his involvement in her brother's murder.

"Ooooh, daddy," she moaned, slumped face-first on the mattress, enjoying the aftermath of a phenomenal orgasm.

"You okay?" Face inquired, rolling over on his back.

"Ooooww, shit yeah! I'm good, daddy," she assured, catching her breath.

She caught her breath, then cuddled in Face's arms.

"I'm sorry to hear about'cha brother," Face lied, kissing KoKo's forehead and gripping her soft, succulent ass cheeks.

"Look, Face, I appreciate'chu consoling me, but'chu don't have to. You forgot, I'ma gangsta? My brother was in the life, and it's only two thangz come wit' that. I made my peace wit' it. I'm okay. But what'chu can do is tell me why the fuck you nutted in my face and left me in that room?" she implored, her expression exasperated.

"I had all kinda shit runnin' through my mind, but I apologize. You didn't deserve that," Face explained concisely.

This gesture turned KoKo's frown to a smile.

"It's okay, daddy, I forgive you," she retorted, rubbing Face's chest and wrapping her thighs across Face.

"For the record, I didn't mean to shoot'chu. I was just coming to git my man and shit got thick," Face lied.

"It's alright, daddy. We ain't gotta speak on this no more. I'm just happy you out," KoKo admitted, kissing Face's chest.

"Fasho."

"Answer me this. You fuckin' Lexus now?"

"Lexus? Fuck no! Lexus my homie, we just bool."

"Bool my ass! You mean to tell me you ain't put that dick on her?"

Face shook his head no.

"I know you, Face. That bitch ain't answer yo phone talkin' spicy for nothin'. You put that dick on that hoe," KoKo proclaimed.

"Maaaan! Where my son at?" Face inquired, changing the subject.

"He wit' my sister," she countered, then started placing tender wet kisses down Face's chest.

"I wanna see'em."

"Okay, daddy," KoKo assured in between kisses, making her way down to Face's dick and eating him like the true man-eater that she was.

Face gripped the sheets while his toes curled and fought for dear life to keep KoKo from sucking the soul from his body. The next morning, when Face awoke, KoKo was gone.

Chapter 11
Spin Back

After washing KoKo's scent from his flesh, Face hopped out of the shower and got dead fresh. He dipped in Louis, sprayed Creed all over his body, then hopped in his K5 and headed to his mother's. When he pulled up, Sierra approached before he could put the car in park.

"Wassup, brother?" Sierra greeted, leaning in Face's window.

"You want some seafood?" she inquired.

"Hell yeah!"

"Run to the store for me right quick, please!"

"For what?"

"I need some butter, garlic, lemon juice, and a case of eggs," Sierra proclaimed.

"Aight, where the money?" Face asked, holding out his hand.

"Boy, don't play wit' me! Hurry up too."

"Where World and everybody at?"

"They was all just here! World, TJ, and B3. They all jumped in a lil hoopty and left. I'on know…nah, gone head on to the store, boy," Sierra demanded, going back inside.

Face put his car in reverse and headed to Wal-Mart. He found a parking spot close to the front and hopped out with his jewels on.

"Damn, so that's how you do all the women who give you they number?" an angelic voice implored.

Face looked up and smiled, surprised.

"Kayla? Awl man. It ain't like that, ma. I been dealing wit' a lot of shit. I was gone hit'chu after I dealt wit' all that," Face explained, closing the space between them.

"Understood, but you still can call to vent. I'ma real good listener," Kayla enunciated, looking at Face up and down intently.

"In that case, I'ma be hittin' yo line soon," he assured, grabbing both of her hands.

"Promise?" Kayla asked in a vivacious tone.

Face smiled before replying, "I promise."

He retorted by kissing her on the cheek and forehead.

"Oooow, look at'chu! Done got ma lil coda pop wet and stuff. Let me get away from you, 'cause, uh…uh!" Kayla pronounced, walking away from Face.

He chuckled.

"I'ma hit'cha line," Face yelled.

Kayla threw thumbs up while putting tremendous space between them. Face headed inside and grabbed a buggy. The moment he placed the eggs inside the cart, his phone rang.

"Yeah!"

"Hey, friend," Lexus greeted, with good vibes dripping from her voice.

"Lex, wassup, ma?"

"I was just callin' to check on you. I haven't heard from you since the last time you were here and was wondering if I could see you tonight."

"Listen Lex. After what'chu did for me, I'ma always make time for you. You hear me?"

Face could feel Lexus smiling through the phone.

"Okay, baby, I'm here. Just pull up," Lexus pronounced, excited.

"Fasho!" Click!

"Heey, Face!" a voice called out behind him.

When he turned around he noted it was CeeCee, KoKo's sister.

64

"Nawl! CeeCee, girl, wass poppin'?" Face asked, a lil skeptical about CeeCee's take on him almost killing her sister.

"Other than my brother gettin' killed, I'm makin' it."

"Yeah, I'm sorry to hear that," Face lied.

"All good. You know Suga Mama bred straight gangstas. This shit built Ford tough, nigga," CeeCee boasted.

"I hear you," Face asserted, slightly amazed.

CeeCee gazed at Face a few moments with no words spoken, then busted up the silence.

"You know, I know you almost killed my sister, right?" CeeCee mentioned, crossing her arms across her chest.

"Yeah, I figured that much," Face admitted.

"Don't trip though. She let it be known what she did to you, and how you didn't know she was in the car. At least that's the story she tells. Face, when I met'chu, I tried to tell you my sister wasn't shit! I tried to get'chu to choose me, and maybe this could have been yo' baby," CeeCee articulated, picking a baby up out of its car seat that she had in the buggy.

Face squinted his eyes and zoomed in on the baby.

"Da fuck?" Face muttered, opening a message that KoKo had sent him.

"This him?" Face asked, showing CeeCee the picture of a baby that KoKo sent him.

"Yeah, that's my baby. How you get that?" CeeCee implored.

All Face could do was shake his head.

"This slimey azz hoe," he muttered, leaving the buggy in the store.

***

Scared of who? / Niggaz pussy like Betty Boop /My lil niggas was itchin' for a body / So I let 'em loose /Yeen on nothin' / tell da truth / when I got to spinnin' / you gone tell

the suits /You just one on the computer / I'ma barracuda /Pop out Uber / get to steppin' in the name of Luger /
The sounds of Big Khufu blared in a hoopty that World had rented from one of his customers. It was thirty minutes after ten p.m., and he had TJ driving with B3 in the backseat trying to spot somethin'. TJ made a left on 13th and Avenue K, noting that there wasn't a soul in sight.

"Man, these bitch-ass niggaz fake!" World snapped, grabbing his phone and calling Amp through Facebook.

"Wass crakin', opp-ass nigga!" Amp answered on Facetime.

Amp was one of C-Rock's lil homies who was in the club the other night. He had been stalking World's page, sending threats with the promise of executing them.

"Maaaan! You niggaz flaugin'! We bendin' all through this shit, you niggaz scared to pop out! On gang we here! Wass poppin', nigga!" World asserted.

"Spin back round! On Dre, nigga, I'm in the middle of the road sticked up!" Amp barked, putting it on his dead homie that he was outside and ready to rack or die.

"I seen you niggaz! Spin back one more time," Amp added excitedly.

"Man, I got a job interview in the morning," TJ interjected.

World quickly ended the Facetime call with a screw face.

"Nigga! What the fuck is you on? We live on Facebook, and you gone say some sucka shit like that?" World implored, seething.

"Yeah mane, you trippin' fa' real!" B3 added.

"Nigga, stop playin' and spin back through that shit!" demanded World.

"Nawl man, I'm fa' real! I gotta job interview in the morning," TJ declared.

"Da fuck you jump in the whip for then?" World questioned.

TJ remained silent with a goofy, shameful expression.

"Damn mane, he been fakin' all this time?" B3 inquired. World shook his head in disgust.

"Man, I'ma drop you off to yo sister house on 15th Street. Me and 3 gone go put this work in, then swang back to get 'chu. I ain't gone fuck up ya lil interview. Pull over, man, I'm drivin'. All this motion we got, you wanna fuckin' nine-to-five... pull over man!" World ordered.

"I'ma go on the next one, bra," TJ promised, pulling over.

"Nawl nigga, stay out the way and keep ya lil job," World added, stepping out of the passenger side while TJ stepped out of the driver's side.

"Come back and get me when y'all done," TJ pronounced.

Boc! Boc! World put two shots in TJ's face, dropping him in front of the murder bucket proficiently. Boc! Boc! Boc! Already peeping the play, B3 planted three more in TJ's chest, then continued to the passenger's side. World shook his head in disappointment and hopped in the driver's seat. He then put the car in drive and ran TJ's body over before vanishing into the night under a bloody moon.

Chapter 12
Cry Blood

"Man, stop hittin' my fuckin' line! Hoe, you dead to me!" Face snapped.

"Oh my God! Face, what did I do? Please just talk to me," KoKo cried, pleading her case hysterically.

"Cry blood, bitch!" Face replied vehemently.

Click! Face hung up on KoKo and downed the shots that World had ordered for him.

They were at the Hill-top taking shots and catching plays.

"Still fuckin' wit' that crazy bitch," World said, shaking his head. "If I ever catch that bitch, I'ma kill 'a, on gang!" promised World.

"I ain't trippin', homie," Face assured, sending KoKo to voicemail.

"Aight! I'm dead ass! You act like ya heart in the way of smushin' the hoe, so I'ma facilitate that play," World added, his phone ringing seconds later.

He seen that it was Amp calling through Facebook.

"Step outside wit' me," World told Face.

Face followed World outside the bar with his hand inside his right pocket, clutching his pistol.

"Wass poppin'?" Face implored, looking around the parking lot.

World shook his head from side to side and pointed at his phone before answering.

"Wass poppin', Gangsta? I been lookin' for you, but can't manage to spot 'cha," World proclaimed, smirking devilishly.

"All Kapp! You know where I'm at. My location live as we speak, kapped-put-ass nigga!" Amp snarled.

"I hear ya nigga!"

"Yeah, I know it. I know, I can't play wit'cha, I gotta gone step on ya! I seen how you did ya own homie! I heard fooly tell you he ain't wanna spin and you stepped on buddy! Ya own homie!" Amp proclaimed.

"I'on know what'chu talkin' 'bout, but I'll definitely be through there to holla at 'cha," World added.

"You got the location! All that rappin' you doin', come drop that album! Studio open twenty-four seven."

Click! Amp hung up in World's face.

"Who the fuck was that?" implored Face.

"One of them lil niggaz from the club the other night. I guess he found my page and been trollin' me every since."

"What homeboy he talkin' 'bout?" Face questioned.

"You don't view TC Palms, nigga?" World stated sardonically.

Face pondered a moment before it hit him.

"TJ?" Face asked dubiously.

"Right," World retorted, folding his arms across his chest.

"For what?" Face wanted to know.

"He showed weakness when we went to go drill. TJ showed me that he'll tell somethin'. I can't and won't chance my freedom on a nigga who ain't solid!"

Face shook his head in agreement.

"I'on want to, but I had to, fam," World explained. "B3 was wit' me. He put work in too. I like 'em. Keep him around," World asserted.

"Okay 3," Face muttered, shaking his head up and down.

"So, what we gone do 'bout fool who stalkin' ya line?" questioned Face.

"Plate 'em! All them niggaz is plates!" World affirmed.

***

Lexus pulled on the side of the road in front of the 17th Street store by the roundabout and hopped out in a pair of skin-tight Etchika shorts and tank top. Her cameltoe protruded provocatively, enticing all that laid eyes upon it.

"Hey guys!" Lexus snickered before walking into the store.

A gang of youngins followed her into the store hounding and shooting their shot.

"Aye ma, whateva you getting' on me," said a youngin named Byrd.

"Nawl, fuck that, I got 'cha lil baby," another one added, named Calico.

"Is that right?" Lexus retorted, smiling, her hazel eyes tantalizing.

"Hell yeah," they yelled in unison.

"Well, get me a few Grab-A-Leafs and some Newports," Lexus proclaimed.

"Aye, Steve, put her shit on my tab," C-Rock voiced from behind them all.

Lexus turned to see who had picked the tab up.

"Okay, my friend!" The Arab pronounced, handing Lexus her items.

"Thank you!" she asserted seductively.

"Come on, let me walk you out," C-Rock offered.

"Man, you cock-blockin'," Byrd voiced.

"Watch ya mouth lil nigga," C-Rock warned, opening the door for Lexus.

When they stepped outside, C-Rock guided her to his truck, reached in the window, and pulled out an ounce of white cap.

"Here lil mama," C-Rock handed her the weed.

"Thank you!"

"No problem. Let me walk you to yo car," he volunteered.

All his youngins were right behind him, gawking.

"That's okay, I'm finna pull into the parking lot and chill a lil bit anyway," Lexus enunciated, walking to her vehicle.

"Damn, them cheeks hangin' out dem lil shorts," Amp yelled.

Even though Lexus told them she was only heading to her car to pull into the store, they all made their way to her car. On key, the back door swung open, and Face stepped out with a .308 blackout, spitting .308s from right to left like a painter's brush to canvas. Face hit every target standing by Lexus's car, spinning and dropping them artistically. He then stepped back into the backseat, and Lexus pulled off smoothly into the night.

A second car pulled up with a beautiful redbone driving by the name of Ashley. World and B3 bounced out of the passenger and backseat with FN's and stood over the bodies that were still moving.

"Aaaahh!" Amp cried, attempting to crawl away but only moving in place.

"Nah, this how you drop an album, ana?"

Boc! Boc! Boc! World had the gun so close to Amp's face that blood saturated it and dripped from the barrel.

"Bitch-ass nigga," World added.

Boc! Boc! Boc! Boc! B3 put four holes in C-Rock's face, then trotted back to the whip with World behind him.

"Let's roll, bae," World told Ashley.

She slipped away swiftly into the night, leaving a nightmare on 17th Street.

Chapter 13
Don't Add Up

"17th STREET MASSACRE... FOUR SLAIN!" Lexus read on the sheriff's Facebook page while on Facetime with Face.

She was sitting on her porch, smoking a joint, feeling optimistic about her role in the murders. Lexus felt as if risking her life for Face would bring them closer, and she was right.

"NO SUSPECTS AT THIS TIME!!" Lexus continued to read.

"You know this makes us bonded by murder," Face informed.

"Yes, I do. Face, I'll do anything for you. All you gotta do is ask," Lexus proclaimed, taking a pull from her blunt.

"What'chu tellin' me? You love me?" Face implored.

"I do. I think I loved you ever since the threesome we had with KoKo," she admitted, smiling majestically.

"I respect it. Truthfully, I can't say I love you, but I do care about 'chu. I respect you and honor your friendship. Nah, if you ask me do I perceive me falling in love wit'chu in the near future, hell yeah. You solid and loyal... that's all it take to win my heart," Face articulated.

"That's good enough for me. I'll take it," Lexus asserted happily.

"You know the vibe."

"Of course. So, can I see you anytime today?"

"Yeah, I just gotta handle somethin' then I'm in ya chest."

"Okay, I'm here baby," Lexus proclaimed, standing and walking to the edge of her porch.

"You need anything?"

"Just you, Face," she retorted genuinely.

"Aight, later ma."

"Later." Click!

Lexus inhaled deeply and exhaled slow. Face was always the type of nigga she'd dreamed of… Driven, understanding, solid, and dangerous. She was more than confident that she would capture Face's heart sooner than later.

Hearing the ice cream truck, she looked up and seen it coming down the street. A lady and her kids stopped the truck a few apartments down from Lexus, so she decided to make her way over for her purchase. She had been craving salt-n-vinegar chips and a pickled sausage for days now. Lexus was a light-skinned beauty who loved to wear attire that left little to the imagination, so niggas was always shootin' they shot everywhere she went.

"Hey, there slim!" an older man named Buga Suga yelled as Lexus stepped into the street to cross over.

"Heey, Buga—!"

BAM! Before she could finish speaking to Buga Suga, a gray Chevy S-10 hit Lexus at sixty miles an hour from behind. Her clothes got caught in the axle, causing her to be dragged for an entire block. Women screamed in shock, kids watched perplexed, and a few niggaz who knew Lexus from the hood rushed to be of some assistance—if there was anything left to assist. The driver fled the scene.

***

Face hung his phone up and sat it on the nightstand next to his bed. He thought about Lexus revealing her love for him and took a moment to process his feelings about it. Face's feelings towards Lexus were in an abstruse state due to the manner in which he'd met her.

73

"You okay?" Kayla implored, entering Face's room fresh out of the shower.

After hitting Face's phone up, he invited her over for Netflix and chill, which she kindly accepted with elation.

"Yeah, I'm good. How 'bout you? You comfortable?" he inquired, grabbing a pre-rolled blunt and putting flame to it. Kayla dropped her robe, exposing her celestial body.

"I'm feelin' the hospitality, but I'll be better when you push down in me," she voiced, crawling in the bed and snuggling up under him.

Face hit the blunt then offered it to her.

"Umm uhh! I'm good on that, but I been waiting to smoke this," Kayla asserted, kissing and licking a trail down Face's chest to the base of his dick.

She grabbed Face's dick with her long manicured nails and slipped it in and out of her mouth, an inch deeper every time.

"Ooooohh ssshit!" Face cried, quickly throwing his blunt in an ashtray on the nightstand.

"Ummhmm!" Kayla taunted, twisting and turning her head while massaging Face's dick.

Face clenched his teeth and grabbed her hair like a pair of reins.

"Ffffuck, you eatin' that dick!" he continued to cry.

Face's comment enthused her, sending her performance into overdrive. Kayla bobbed her head expeditiously with purpose until she felt Face's dick grow longer and harder.

"I'm finna skeet, ssss, fffffuck!" he moaned, letting her hair go to grab the Egyptian cotton sheets.

His teeth clenched and his toes curled while Kayla sucked and swallowed all within.

"Mmmm…umm…hmm!" Kayla muttered seductively while Face trembled in euphoria.

"Sssshit!" Face yelled as his orgasm began to subside.

"You taste so good," Kayla asserted, planting kisses on the head of his dick.

"I think I'm in love wit'cha mouth," Face admitted, biting his bottom lip.

"Wait till you get this pussy," she boasted, climbing on top of Face and straddling him.

The moment she grabbed his dick to insert it in her, Face's phone rang. When Face reached for his phone, Kayla grabbed his hand.

"Let it ring, and get in this pussy," she cried.

"I gotta answer that. That's my nigga," he retorted, grabbing the phone and answering it.

"3, wass poppin'?" Face implored.

"I'm outside, mane. Come jump in wit' me. We need to talk," B3 proclaimed.

"Say no moe." Click!

"Look, I'ma get wit'chu later. You gotta roll," Face pronounced, getting out of his bed to get dressed.

Kayla exhaled, slightly irritated, but made her way out of the bed to get dressed as well.

"Why do I feel like you just beat me out my head?" Kayla pouted.

"This ain't that. We gone link," he assured, grabbing his pistol from under the mattress and tucking it.

"Ole, Lord. Let me get up outta here," Kayla stated, grabbing her belongings.

Face walked her to her car, then hopped in with B3.

"What da lick read?" Face greeted, dapping B3 up.

B3 inhaled and exhaled, shaking his head.

"It's all bad, mane. Lexus died today, mane," B3 informed confidently.

Face glanced at B3 in disbelief.

"Fuck you mean?" he implored, his forehead creased.

"Mane, somebody ran her over today on 23rd and kept goin'. Whoever it was dragged her for a whole block, mane. Shit fucked up fareal, mane," B3 pronounced.

"Damn, I just talked wit' her earlier today," said Face, wiping a tear from the corner of his right eye. "So nobody don't know who did it?"

"Nawl, mane, and it wasn't no accident. Them folks was going over sixty miles an hour, mane. Me personally, I think somebody prolly seen us come outta Lexus' house when we stepped on them niggaz, mane. They ain't seen us particularly, but they seen somebody leave out her back door right before the killin's, mane," B3 voiced.

Face shook his head in disagreement.

"Shit don't add up, my nigga. We smushed everything on the porch. Ain't no witnesses and nobody seen us slip outta Lexus' apartment. Shit really coulda been an accident, and the driver prolly had no D.L.'s, fam," Face theorized.

"Listen, mane. I was outside when it happen. I was walking my kids to the ice cream truck when that gray truck came through full speed, mane. I sent the kids back inside and went to check on Lexus, mane. Seeing her like that fucked me up, mane," B3 stressed, shaking his head.

"We gone get to the bottom of it," Face assured, exhaling as he gazed out the passenger window in deep thought.

Chapter 14
Fuck You!

Lexus' funeral was held at Greater New Bethal's Church on the bottom. The crowd was mild, majority being family. She had only a handful of friends due to being an anti-social introvert. Face made his way to her casket, dipped in an all-red Balmain Monogram print denim suit with all his jewelry on. When he made it to her casket, he could see the scars in her face from the hit and run. He stroked her cheek with his index finger, then bent down to kiss her on the cheek.

"You gone always be my ride or die. We foreva bonded through murda," Face whispered in her ear before placing another kiss on her forehead.

He then reached behind his ear, grabbed a blunt, and placed it in her casket.

"Um, um, um!" Someone behind Face cleared their throat rudely.

When Face looked back, he noted KoKo standing there in an all-black Alexander Valtier dress, Paloma Picasso heels, and a blonde lace front that was slayed to perfection. Face's expression was of one who'd bit a lemon. He elevator-eyed her, then stepped off heading outside. B3, who was in the back of the church posted up, followed behind him.

Once Face was outside, he reached for the other blunt behind his other ear and sparked it.

"You aight, mane?" B3 asked, sparking a Newport.

Face shook his head yeah.

"Wassup, Face?" KoKo implored audaciously.

Face glanced at KoKo, then quickly turned away from her, continuing to smoke his blunt.

"Oh, so you can whisper and kiss on that dead hoe, but'chu can't speak to me? Really, Face?" KoKo implied, envy dripping from her voice.

"Maaaan! Fuck ass hoe!" Face barked, snatching his FN 502 from his Balmain's and placing it in the middle of her forehead.

KoKo didn't flinch. Instead, she narrowed her eyes with a dark expression on her face.

"Where the fuck my son at, hoe?" Face asked, even though he knew she had lied to him about being pregnant.

"Do you, nigga," KoKo dared in a calm but threatening tone as tears cascaded down her cheeks.

Boc! Boc! Boc! Face let off three shots, but B3 had knocked his arm away from KoKo's face, then restrained Face with a bear hug and walked him towards the car.

"You trippin, mane! Not here, mane! Come on, let's go before them folks get here, mane," B3 enunciated.

Face knew B3 was right, so he obliged and made his way to the passenger seat, gazing at KoKo the whole time. KoKo returned the gaze, never batting an eyelash.

"I love you, nigga!" she yelled from the church's stairs before Face closed the passenger's door.

"That bitch crazy, mane. I told you years ago KoKo was gone take you up through there, mane," B3 asserted, shaking his head.

"Man, fuck you," Face muttered.

***

KoKo sat in her truck and rolled a molly joint in the back of Cee Cee's apartment in the projects. Once she finished rolling the blunt, she sparked it and inhaled deeply. The taste of the cigarette and molly mixture galvanized her taste buds and shifted her mind into a state of bliss as she exhaled. Memories of her and Face pervaded her mind, prompting tears to fall rapidly from the wells of her eyes.

The molly had KoKo extremely emotional. She knew that she'd done some villainous things to Face, but still she loved him gravely. Composing herself, she wiped her tears and made an exit from her vehicle to the back door of Cee Cee's apartment.

When she entered, Cee Cee was over the stove cooking oxtails and mac-n-cheese. KoKo took a toke from her blunt and blew smoke in the air carelessly.

"Wassup, sis?" KoKo greeted, taking a seat at the kitchen table.

"KoKo, why is you smokin' that shit in here when you know my baby in here?" Cee Cee snapped.

"Not right nah, Cee Cee, please! Yo baby is way over there, he okay. I'm goin' through it right nah. Just please leave me alone."

"What the hell wrong wit'chu?" Cee Cee implored.

KoKo exhaled, seething.

"I just got into it with Face. He pulled a gun on me and asked me about his son. Girl, he is so fuckin' mad at me," KoKo proclaimed.

"He pulled a gun on you?"

"Umm hmm!" KoKo retorted.

Cee Cee shook her head.

"Oh, I forgot to tell you. I seen him in Wal-Mart the other day. He seen me and my baby, then pulled out his phone and showed me a picture. He asked who baby I had wit' me?" Cee Cee explained.

"What did you say?" KoKo questioned, putting the blunt out in an ashtray.

"I told'em it was my baby."

"Why the fuck would you do that? I told you to stick to the plan until I was ready to tell'em! Damn!" KoKo barked.

"KoKo, I am not finna be playin' games wit' my baby. That's out!" Cee Cee snapped, putting the lid back over the crock pot and heading to the living room to have a seat on her couch next to her baby who was in a baby seat.

Ponderous moments passed by before KoKo took a deep breath and exhaled with exasperation.

"You know what, I apologize. I'm dead ass wrong," KoKo admitted.

"You straight," Cee Cee assured, changing her TV app from Hulu to BET Plus.

"You mind if I use your charger? My phone bout dead," asked KoKo.

"Yeah, it's in the kitchen by the crock pot. Just take my phone off and bring it to me."

"Okay," KoKo said, standing to go retrieve Cee Cee's phone.

After getting the phone and charger, she headed over to Cee Cee.

"Here," pronounced KoKo, handing Cee Cee her phone.

Cee Cee grabbed her phone, then directed her attention back to her show *Zatima*.

"Bitch!" KoKo yelled through clenched teeth, wrapping the phone charger cord around Cee Cee's neck.

Cee Cee's first instinct reaction was to claw at the cord, attempting to remove it from around her neck.

"If you woulda kept yo fuckin' mouth closed, Face wouldn't be mad at me," she sneered, pulling the cord tight as she could as tears fell from her face.

Cee Cee fought hard to chase her breath but to no avail. Her life was slipping away rapidly.

"All you had to do was keep yo fuckin' mouth closed, and you couldn't do that. It's like you just said fuck me…but nall, bitch. It's fuck you, hoe! Fuck you! Fuck you! Fuck you, bitch!" KoKo barked through clenched teeth as Cee Cee's soul left her body to be recycled with that infinite energy that never dies.

KoKo waited until a little after three a.m. to put the baby in her truck. She went back inside to clean all that she had touched, then slipped away unseen, leaving Cee Cee to be found by whoever.

Chapter 15
Whateva!

"My nigga, it's been a brazy week, fareal," Face voiced after taking a shot from a bottle of Don Julio.

"Shid, it is what it it's suppose to be. It just another day at life, ya feel me? We havin' extraordinary motion! We sleepin' on niggaz! Plus ween been unalived yet! Enjoy each moment as it transpire, my nigga," World articulated.

"Talk that shit, mane," B3 added, feeling good and tipsy.

Face heard them, but he wasn't listening. His thoughts were on KoKo when his phone rang. Looking at his phone, he couldn't believe who was calling from Facebook.

"Hey, Face," Terrel replied. "Look, I know we haven't spoken in a while, but I need to have a conversation wit'chu in person," she expressed with urgency.

"I'm at my mama spot, pull up."

"Okay, I'ma few minutes away. See you in a few." Click!

"Who was that?" World questioned.

"Terrell," Face informed, taking another shot before sparking a blunt.

"Nawl, she want her baby back," clowned World.

"I doubt that. I took her through hell," Face admitted, blowing smoke from his nose.

"What else she want then?" World implored, using his outstretched arms for emphasis.

Face shrugged his shoulders while gazing off in the distance.

"Let me hit that blunt, mane," B3 asked.

Face shook his head no, then pulled a quarter from his Billionaire Boy sweats and handed it to 3.

In that moment a white Tesla with tinted windows rounded the corner. World and B3 clutched their weapons as the vehicle pulled in the driveway. The driver let the window down.

"Don't shoot my car up. I just got it," Terrell pronounced.

"Wassup, T?" World spoke.

Terrell waved. Face walked to her window.

"How you been?" Face questioned, then hit his blunt.

Terrell reached for Face's blunt and took it from his grasp. She then took a deep pull and exhaled.

"Jump in, we need to talk," Terrell stated.

"Oh. So I gotta have a moose knuckle to hit yo blunt, mane?" B3 clowned.

Face ignored B3 and hopped in the passenger's side. They shared a gaze before Face broke the silence.

"So what brings you back to me?" Face implored, noticing how gorgeous and thick Terrell had gotten.

"It's somethin' I want'chu to hear," she asserted, grabbing her phone.

Once she found what she was looking for, she pressed play and handed the phone to Face.

Terrell: "Hold on, I was textin' my homegirl, I ain't hear you. What'chu said?"

Varis: "I said, I just found out the nigga that killed my cousin beat that shit. That pussy ass nigga out, and I'ma spank that boy! On gang!"

Terrell: "What'chu mean spank'em and who you talkin' bout?"

Varis: "Face! That bitch ass nigga killed my cousin Pooh Bear over that hoe! I'ma kill'em, on my mama. I gotta have boy!"

Terrell: "Aye, check this out! See, like you gotta lotta shit goin' on wit'chu, and I'on want that type of energy round me, playa. You gotta get the fuck out my shit! Right nah!"

Varis: "What'chu talkin' bout? What'chu mean get out? I thought we was goin' to the American Legion tonight."

Terrell: "Look, I'll see you there, but'chu gotta go!"

Terrel ended the recording.

"Who that is?" Face questioned, unbothered.

"Some nigga I was talkin' to for bout a month, name Varis," Terrell said, grabbing her phone from Face.

She went to the photo gallery and showed Face a picture of Varis.

"Yeah, I know that police ass nigga," Face asserted.

"Look, I'on care nothing bout 'em. You see, once he said yo name, I made his ass leave," she announced, her voice stern.

"Yeah, I love that shit. Do me a favor and delete that recording."

"Okay. Whateva else you need me to do, it's whateva," Terrell mentioned.

Face looked into her enchanting eyes, then slid his hand between her thighs, up under her Balenciaga skirt. Rubbing his middle and index fingers across her clit and swollen labium, he felt the warmth and dampness through her Prada panties. The fatness of her pussy sent chills throughout Face's body.

"Whateva?" he implied, smiling mischievously.

Terrell grabbed Face's fingers and guided them inside her warm, wet canal.

"Whateva," she assured.

***

Later that night, a mild breeze drifted under a clear sky full of stars. Traffic was semi-rowdy due to clubs letting out, and the car Face was driving appeared to be out of commission on the side of 19th Street. Nobody stopped to offer a hand while he meddled under the hood.

A car with a screaming sound system crept up the block and stopped next to Face due to a long line in traffic. Face looked to his right and noted a sky-blue Oldsmobile sitting in 28's.

Dipped in all black—a turtleneck, black Dickies, a black skully, and a black Corona mask—Face grabbed the AK he had under the hood, turned it toward the Oldsmobile, and fired. 7.62 rounds tore through the glass and metal like butter, Swiss-cheesing the unknown female passenger and Varis in the driver's seat.

Face walked up on the passenger side and continued to spray while cars scattered every which way, trying to avoid the crossfire. When Face was satisfied, he jumped into the backseat behind the driver. The getaway car pulled off and disappeared into traffic, leaving glass, metal, and carnage for the public's eyes.

Chapter 16
Yes, Lawd! Lawd, Yes!

The sounds of Friday's *Back to You* serenaded Terrell's room while Face slow-stroked her from behind aggressively and deep. Terrel gripped her Armani pillow with both hands while Face kissed, licked, and sucked on her ears, neck, and shoulders all while still stroking her proficiently.

"Oooooowww, yeessss, daddy! Get this pussy," Terrell sang like a Primadonna through clenched teeth.

"This what'chu want?" Face whispered in her ear, switching his motion to a slow, hard Jamaican grind.

"Ssss…Aaaaahh, fuck yeah! Ssss…Oooowww, baby, I missed you," she cried cumming for the second time.

Face felt her getting wetter while her walls clenched around him. "Ffffuuck!" he groaned, grabbing her by her hips, forcing her to position herself on her knees with a deep arch in her back. Face rose to his knees, put a dip in his back, and proceeded to stroke Terrell rapidly and violently.

"Ssss, ffffuck! Right there, sss, ooh, ssshit! Right there, daddy, yes!" she cried, gripping her purple thousand-count sheets. "Fuck this pussy good!"

"Ummhmm, nut on this dick!"

Smack!

Face slapped Terrell's soft ass with the proper amount of pressure, causing her to cum profusely.

"Damn, this pussy skeetin'," Face stated as he seen her creaming over him with each stroke.

"Oh my God! Sss...hhhaaaah!" Terrell cried while trembling.

Face grabbed her by her shoulders and gave her all that he had, prompting a smacking sound to echo throughout the house.

"Sssss, ooow, I'm finna nut again," she moaned.

Face slipped out of her, pulled her to the edge of the bed, then slipped his hands under her from behind. He gripped her by her waist and stood up, causing her to be upside down with her ass and pussy directly in his face. Terrell placed her hand on his knees for stability and began to suck Face's dick artistically. They both moaned while they ate each other up savagely. When Terrell felt her flood gates opening, she sucked Face's dick more aggressively, forcing him to cum with her. He turned his back towards the bed and eased down on it, laying on his back with Terrell's ass still in his face. He leaned up and placed tender kisses on her ass cheeks while she continued to suck the rest of the nut out of Face.

"Ummm," she moaned.

"Aight, fuck! That's enough," Face declared.

Terrell whined but complied with Face's wishes. She kissed the head of his dick, then turned around and laid on his chest. After catching her breath, Terrell got up to go clean herself and grabbed a warm washcloth to clean Face off, too.

"That was so good," Terrell admitted, wiping Face's dick clean.

"Hell yeah. I miss you," Face added.

Terrell sat the rag on the nightstand then cuddled up under Face. "I miss you more," she retorted. rubbing Face's chest.

Face placed a kiss on her forehead. "Look, I appreciate what'chu did for me. That nigga coulda caught me slippin."

"You know I gotcha. Even though you hurt my feelins, I wouldn't be able to live wit' myself if I didn't put'chu on point."

"I respect it, but'chu know I was fresh out on some other shit. No excuses, though. I apologize. You forgive me?" he implored with a smile.

"Come on nah. I was a getaway driver, and I gave you some of this good pussy…nigga you know the vibe," Terrell enunciated.

"I just wanted to hear you say it. On some real shit, though, what happened tonight is to neva be mentioned, ever! Understand?" Face implored seriously.

"Understood, daddy."

"Aight."

"So, what about us?" Terrell questioned.

"How you mean?"

"I wanna try us again. You been out for a while now, everything you wanted to explore should have been explored by now," she explained, eyeing him shrewdly.

Face took in all that she conveyed while gazing at her perfect white teeth contrasted sharply by her smooth, almost Black, skin and perfectly proportioned body. "Us again, huh?" he implied.

"Ummhmm. I know about everything you've been through with KoKo, and I just wanna show you that, that ain't it. This is where it's at, over here. Let me love you, Face," she persisted.

With clock-like precision, Face rolled on top of Terrell and kissed her passionately from her mouth to down south.

"Is that a yes?" Terrell managed in between gasp.

"What'chu think?" Face implored, latching on Terrell's clit, sending her into a blissful state.

***

"Bae!" Terrell called out for the fourth time to Face who appeared to be in a blissful sleep. Bae!" she called once more, standing in front of her queen size bed.

Face slipped out of whatever dream he was having and opened his eyes. When his vision cleared, he noted Terrell standing parrot-toed with a tray in her hands. "Damn," he muttered, viewing the perfectly fitting Etchika shorts that hugged her camel toe snuggly.

Her pussy print wasn't oversized nor to minute, but rather flawlessly proportioned. She was slim-thick with an extremely flat stomach.

"I made you shrimp, fish, and Cajun grits, baby," she said smiling, chortling, knowing what Face was gawking at.

"Spin around for me one time, boo bae," Face requested.

Terrell turned her back towards him and locked her legs, making her cheeks even.

"Yes, lawd! Lawd, yes! Damn, bae, that gap is everything!" Face voiced, loving how Terrell's ass cheeks sat perfectly with her passionfruit sitting elegantly between them like a Chinese plum. "I think I love you, no Kapp!" Face clowned sitting up.

"Stop playin' wit' my emotions," Terrell asserted, spinning around to bring Face his breakfast. She walked to Face's side of the bed.

"Hold that tray up for me a minute," he demanded.

Terrell complied. Face slid her Etchika to the side, swiped his tongue across her clit, then placed a wet tender kiss between her lips.

"Sss, boy! You gone make me drop this tray! Here nah, stop playin' if you ain't gone finish," she stated, pushing the tray towards Face, forcing him to take it.

He laughed, knowingly grabbing the tray. "I appreciate'chu, fareal," he admitted, diving into the food.

"No problem," she retorted, kissing Face on his cheek. "I gotta jump in this shower and get ready for my appointments."

"For what?"

"Hair, nails, and spa day," she admitted.

"Okay," Face pronounced.

"You need anything before I jump in this water?"

"I'm good, sexy," Face assured, stuffing his face.

"Okay, daddy," she said before heading to the shower.

Face reached for his phone that was on silent and seen that he had multiple missed calls from KoKo and B3. He decided to call B3 on Facetime.

"Wassup mane?" B3 answered.

"Wass poppin', 3?" Face asked, devouring the fish and shrimp.

"Look, mane, I need you to pop out, mane. Come fuck wit' me, mane."

"Talk to me," Face proclaimed.

"Mane, I ain't got no mo' Ps, mane! Shit gone, and deez folks on my line, mane. On top of that, mane, they found Cee Cee dead in her apartment," B3 explained.

"Nawl!" Face added in disbelief.

"Yeah, mane. Say she was strangled, and it look like whoever did it trashed the spot. They don't know who got her baby neither, mane. Shit wild!"

"Everybody dying round this bitch. Damn, let me get dressed, then you gone smell me in a few," Face disclosed.

"Aight, mane, pull up.

"Already!" Face retorted. *Click!*

Chapter 17
A.M.G.

After pulling up on Moses, Face paid what he owed, grabbed twenty more pounds, and was headed to B3 when his phone rang.

"Wass poppin'?" Face answered.

"Niggaz like me and you," Assata retorted.

"All the time."

"Pull up, I'm at the spot," Assata stated.

"Say no moe," Face asserted, hanging the phone up.

Instead of heading to B3, he stopped by his spot to drop the work off before heading to Assata's. When Face hopped out of his K5 dipped in an all-red Maison Margiela track suit, lil Fif God and Shooter were on post as usual. They peaced him up, then let him by, surprisingly without a pat-down. Face knocked, then entered the apartment. He noted Assata taking a baby to the back room. She remained hidden for a few minutes, then returned wearing a tight-fitted Chanel dress that matched her red dreads.

"Wass poppin'?" Assata implored, sitting in a red-leathered lazy boy.

"That five," Face retorted, having a seat across from her on a red sectional.

Assata nodded her head in approval.

"I need you to po' me a drink or somethin', and don't lie to me," Assata enunciated, her voice thick.

"Shoot," he replied.

"You had somethin' to do wit' Knight?" Assata questioned, observing Face's expressions and body language.

"So, they say," he shot back, looking her in her eyes.

"So, they say, huh?" Assata voiced, sparking a blunt. "You know he the homie, right? He G.K.B.," she added, blowing smoke from her nose.

"I'm O-50."

"You know yo' 21 Gunz?" she implored.

"Bronx," Face retorted, meaning yes.

"Then you know if you plated him without proper protocol, that a double-o-banga, right?"

"Like I said, I'm O-50," Face proclaimed, his demeanor calm as a lake.

Assata noted how he didn't admit or deny the allegations against him.

"Well, everybody knew his jersey was dirty anyway. It ain't no real proof, it's all hearsay."

"Exactly," Face added. Assata eyed Face for a few moments before speaking.

"Lil Fif God and Shooter put twenty more plates in yo' trunk. Same ticket."

"Aight," Face retorted.

"One more thing before you leave," Assata added, putting the roach out in an ashtray.

"Anything, Queen," Face stated.

Assata uncrossed her legs and opened them wide, placing each leg over an arm of the chair. Face's excitement and heartrate increased as he noted she had no panties on. Assata's pussy was extremely gorgeous and taste-ready. With a clear understanding between the two, Face kneeled before her, placed his hands on the back of her knees, and pinned them to her chest. He placed kisses and sucked her inner thighs on both sides before becoming face-to-face with her place of happiness. He placed a kiss on her clit.

"Sss, whooo," Assata moaned, noting how soft Face's lips were.

He swiped his tongue from the bottom to the top of her clit, then blew softly, sending chills throughout her body. Face then flattened out his tongue and placed it on her clit, moving from left to right slowly, picked up the pace, then slowed it once more. Goin' in for the kill, Face latched on her clit, sucking, licking, and blowing until Assata saturated his mouth with an abundance of pussy juice.

"Oh my God," Assata cried, trembling while creaming in Face's mouth.

"Ummhmmm," Face added, swallowing all that she dripped.

"Fffffuck," she moaned, rolling her hips and throwing her pussy in his face until her orgasm subsided.

Face's dick was harder than Superman's kneecaps. He wiped his mouth, then stood, preparing to slip his dick from his Margielas. Assata cuffed his balls, then fondled the length and girth of Face's dick while standing.

"Impressive! Not today though, bloody," she pronounced, kissing him on the cheek.

Instead of questioning her or feeling played, Face just smirked with docility. After freeing him from a potential life sentence, Face would do any and everything for Assata, including pulling up just to eat on her and dip.

"Respect. Anytime, ya hear me?" Face voiced, heading for the door.

"Woop!"

"Woop!" he replied, leaving the apartment.

***

Face backed into B3's driveway and hopped out, watching everything around him. He noted a crowd of people again mourning at KoKo's mother's apartment. B3 stepped off his porch and greeted Face, who was leaning on his car.

"Was good, mane," B3 implored, dapping Face up.

"Just another day at life, homie," Face philosophized, walking to the back of the trunk.

"Fucked up what happen to Cee Cee, mane," B3 asserted, shaking his head from left to right.

"It is, but don't too much of nothin' surprise me no moe," Face added, placing his foot up under the bumper.

The trunk of his car popped instantly.

"What the fuck was that, mane?"

"It's a keyless entry. Technology a muthafucka, huh?" Face implied.

"Hell yeah."

Face looked back at B3's girl apartment, then back at B3.

"Why you won't move ya girl in a home away from the 3?" Face questioned.

"Awl mane, I love it round hurr, mane. Ain't nothin' like the 23rd, mane. Eventually I'ma buy her one, but right nah, I'm stackin', mane."

Face shrugged his shoulders.

"Grab both of those duffels. Same thang, homie," Face stated. His phone rang afterwards.

"Sayless, mane," 3 replied, grabbing the work and taking it inside.

"Yeah?" Face answered.

"Wass poppin', militant?" Kream greeted.

"Wass poppin', five?"

"Niggaz like us."

"All the time," Face added.

"Homie, for somebody who just beat a life sentence, you sho'll makin' a lot of noise," Kream voiced, chuckling.

"I'm just puttin' on, movin' accordingly, big homie."

"Speaking of puttin' on, I got the green light for the subset. A.M.G. been officially stumped!" Kream informed, elated.

"Almighty Militant Gangstaz, huh?"

"Ain't no question, and I'm stampin' up the 020!"

"You already know how I'm movin' 'bout'cha, big homie," Face expressed, fidelity in his heart.

"Facts, homie! Militant we stand! Look, I ain't gone take no moe of ya time, homie. I'ma link later, ya hear me?" Kream pronounced.

"Already!"

"Aight, one!" Click!

B3 approached moments later with two Red Stripes and handed Face one.

"I been thinkin', mane. What'chu gone do wit' KoKo?" 3 asked, worried about his homie.

Face shook his head from left to right.

"Tsss... you know what's brazy, doe? I still love the hoe, but I know I'ma have to step on her," he confessed, shaking his head in self-pity and disgust.

"It's really easy when you balance it out, mane. Just think about all the problems you had since you been outta prison, mane. All this killin' and goin' to jail, mane, all stems from KoKo, man. She not gone leave you alone, mane, so gone put her under, mane," B3 advised.

Face took in all that B3 spilled and knew he was dropping facts.

"I hear you," Face added.

A blue Buick pulled up abruptly with a woman hanging out of the passenger's window. Face and B3 snatched their blix out out of pure instinct.

"You pussy-ass nigga! I should make my nigga get out and beat'chu, bitch boy!" Meka yelled from the car window.

Meka was Kierra's mother and Face's one-time fling.

BOC! BOC! BOC! BOC! Meka ducked her head down under the dashboard.

"Ummhmm!" Face asserted.

BOC! BOC! BOC! BOC! BOC! BOC! Face and B3 knocked the back passengers and the back window completely out and sent a few more through the body of the automobile.

"Stupid-ass hoe!" Face yelled. "I'm gone, homie, love!" Face stated, hopping in his whip while B3 picked the shells up and went inside.

Face got in traffic and got missing.

Chapter 18
Love You To Death

In desperate need of a getaway, Face slid out of town to Orlando for a few days with Terrell. KoKo and Kayla had been blowing his phone up with repetition, but he ignored all calls. They were now finishing their meals inside of The Cheesecake Factory.

"Baby, after I use the ladies' room, I'll be ready to leave," said Terrell.

"Aight, ma. You want anything to go?" Face asked.

"Umm, yeah. Can you get me two slices of pineapple cheesecake and some baked ziti, please?"

"Anything for you, T. Come here," Face voiced, placing a kiss on Terrell's lips.

"Thank you, daddy," she retorted, standing to leave.

Face called a waiter over to put Terrell's order in, then stepped outside to smoke a Newport. As soon as he took a pull from the cigarette, his phone rang. It was Kayla calling to Facetime him. "Kayla wass poppin' wit'chu?" Face answered.

"That's what we doin'? You just gone ghost me and ignore my calls?" Kayla complained.

"Nawl, it ain't like that. I been goin' through so much shit. I just needed a lil getaway. I'm outta town, but I'ma pull up soon as I get back," he promised.

"A getaway, huh? So why you ain't asked me if I wanted to come wit'chu?" she pried.

"Look, to be honest wit'chu, I just met'chu and didn't wanna involve you in some shit that might get'chu fucked up," Face explained.

"Trust me, I did my due diligence. I know exactly who you are and what'chu on. You my type of nigga," she admitted.

"Respect. Don't believe all that you hear, ma. Peep, though. When I get back in town, we gotta talk about some things."

"I'm here."

"Aight ma, love. I'ma pull up."

"Okay. Bye, Face," Kayla pronounced, feeling better that she'd heard from him.

Click!

With perfect timing KoKo called in tandem. Face answered. "Da fuck you want?" Face implored irritably.

"Face," KoKo stated calmly, "I'ma need you to listen and hear me clearly. I love you, nigga. I love you more than my next breath. Hear me when I tell you that I love you to death, and I mean literally, nigga. If I can't have you, nobody can flirt. You know how toxic this shit can get, so stop fuckin' playin' wit me, nigga."

Click! Face's phone alerted him that he had a message. When he checked the message, it was a picture of him standing outside the Cheesecake Factory with the caption "GET RID OF THE HOE BEFORE I DO!"

"Da fuck!" Face yelled, looking around the parking lot.

"Everything okay, bae?" Terrell asked concerned.

Face turned to face Terrell and noticed she had grabbed the food. "Yeah, everything Gucci, ma. Let's get up outta here," Face insisted, wrapping his left arm around Terrell and secretly clutching his pistol with his right. He surveyed their surroundings until they came upon Terrell's car. "I'm driving, ma," Face said walking Terrell to the passenger side and opening the door for her.

"Thank you, daddy," she purred getting into the vehicle.

"You already know," he retorted, closing her door. Making his way to the driver's seat, a car pulled up abruptly behind Face. He turned around, lifting his pistol but quickly hid it behind his back when he seen that it was an elderly woman.

"Young man, do you have the time?" she asked, squinting her eyes.

"No, ma'am, I don't," Face lied, wanting her to pull off as quick as possible.

"Okay, thanks anyway," she retorted, pulling off.

Face quickly hopped into the Telsa and got in traffic. When Face looked over at Terrell, he noted the dubious expression on her face.

"You sure it ain't something you wanna tell me, Face?"

"Damn, T, why you keep asking me that? I told you I'm good," he stated, tryin' to sound convincing.

"Because I just seen you pull a gun out and almost unalive that old lady. Plus, you keep lookin' in all three mirrors like somebody following us. Wassup, Face?" she asked, worried about him. He drew in a deep breath then exhaled loudly.

***

Not willing to endanger Terrell's life anymore than he already had, Face headed back to Fort Pierce and took her to her gated community.

"Face, I appreciate'chu tellin' me the truth and you looking out for me, but I'm not scared of that bitch! We can pull up on that hoe together, right nah!" Terrell snapped.

"Look, it ain't just her. I'm finna pull up on all the women I been dealin' wit and let'em know the shit we had is dead flies. I'm rockin' wit'chu."

Terrell smiled. "Really?" she asked.

"Facts. I'm takin yo' whip though. Nah, gone inside, I'll be back," Face proclaimed, leaning over, kissing Terrell passionately.

"Okay, call if you need me," she said grabbing her food and leaving.

Face pulled off and dialed Kayla's number.

"Hello?" Kaylo answered, her voice soft as drug store cotton.

"Where you at?"

"Home, why?"

"Jump in wit' me. I'm finna pull up," Face pronounced.

"Okay, I'll be outside," Kayla retorted.

"Already," he stated ending the call.

Ten minutes later, Face pulled into Madison Kay, a complex for a woman who paid rent according to their income. Normally the complex was crowded and boisterous but for some reason it was quiet and desolate. Face spotted Kayla wearing a tight fitted Prada dress and a pair of slingback Prada pumps. Her red sister locks correlated with her pumps and Prada bag, demonstrating a real fashion statement.

Face let his window down. "You lookin' good," he complimented.

"Face, I figured that was you," Kayla asserted, making her way to the passenger side and getting in. "Thank you. You looking snackish, too."

"You already know," Face replied, putting the vehicle in drive and taking off.

"Ummm, you smell good, too. What that is?" she implored, leaning in closer to get a better smell and placed a kiss on Face's neck.

"Creed," Face said. "I need you to not kiss on me like that. I'm trying to talk to you about somethin'," he added.

"Oh, you wanna talk? Let's talk then," Kayla asserted, snatching Face's dick from his Margiela's and working it into her warm mouth.

Chapter 19
Yo' Turn

Kayla sucked Face's dick all the way to a spot that he had on Taylor's Creek bank. Face had backed in next to the pumphouse and nutted in Kayla's mouth.

"Uh, uh! You gone give me some of this dick," Kayla stated as she continued to suck Face's dick until he was hard again.

"Hold up," Face proclaimed, grabbing Kayla by her sister locks and pulling her mouth away from his dick. He opened his door and walked around to her side with his dick exposed to the night's air. Face opened her door. "Bend that shit over," he demanded.

"Umm!" Kayla moaned, hiking her dress up and bending over in the passenger's seat.

Face reached in his pocket for a rubber and slid it on quickly before sliding in her from behind.

"Ooooww, sshit!" She moaned from the warmth of his exceptional size.

Not in the mood for making love, Face slipped into overdrive instantly, killing Kayla from the back.

"Ooow, that's it! FFFFuuuck me, ssshit!" she yelled while her ass smacked and wobbled recklessly.

Face noted that every time he made contact with Kayla's cheeks a foul stench pervaded his nostrils. *Damn this bitch pussy good and stank,* Face thought to himself. He lifted his nose to the sky then pounded away at Kayla's flesh until he came.

"Awww, ffffuck, baby," Kayla cried, biting her bottom lip while creaming all over Face.

He pulled out of her, snatched the rubber off, and slung it to the ground. On the way to the driver's side, he swiped his finger across his nose to make sure he wasn't tripping. "Damn," he muttered getting into the driver's seat.

"Oh my God, that dick is life," Kayla complimented, smiling irrepressibly.

"I gotta go handle some bidness," Face lied trying to get rid of Kayla.

"Aww," she whined, poking her lip out. "Can you buy me some Rice Hut before you take me home?"

"Yeah, I got'cha," Face assured while still thinking to himself how could Kayla be so beautiful with smelly pussy. He couldn't wait to take a long, hot shower.

Kayla periodically touched on Face, rubbing her hand across his lap and leg, irritating him all the more. "You okay, baby?" she asked, still caressing him.

"I'm Gucci," Face replied, pulling into the parking lot of the Rice Hut.

"I want a twelve-piece honey barbeque with some combination rice, extra eggs."

"Got'cha," Face retorted, hopping out and rushing into the Chinese hut.

"How may I help you please?" The Chinaman implored.

"Let me get ah—"

Boc! Boc! Boc! Boc!

Face ducked and snatched his blik out at the same time. When he rose, Face noted a hooded figure jumping into a gray truck. He ran outside and fired three shots, knocking the taillight out, but the driver slipped away. Face looked inside Terrell's car and seen Kayla slumped over with brain fragments all over the interior. Knowing the Rice Hut had no surveillance footage, he took off running across the street behind an old barber shop and hopped a fence that led him to some run-down apartments. When he felt that he was clear, he pulled out his phone and dialed Terrell's number.

"Hey, daddy! I miss you already," Terrell stated cheerfully.

"Bae, listen. Report the whip stolen right nah! I'ma explain later," Face asserted in a tone that indicated urgency.

"Okay, baby, no problem. You okay?"

"Yeah, I'll be there in a minute." Click! Face hung up and called World.

"Wass poppin', bra?" World answered full of energy.

"Listen, pick me up right nah. I'm walkin' down 27th Street," Face proclaimed, talking faster than normal.

"I'm on 29th, right nah! What part of 27th?" World questioned, making a left on 29th and E.

"By 3 O's!"

"I view you! That's you in that red?"

"Affirmative!"

World pulled up with the passenger door already opened.

Face hopped in and they slipped away. "Take me to that gated community by the college."

"Got'cha, but talk to me! Wass poppin', nigga?" World inquired.

"Maaan, I was wit' the hoe I met in the Elk's."

"Who, Kayla?" World asked.

"Yeah. So, I hit the hoe, and take her to the Rice Hut, I go in to order her food and shots rang out."

"Nawl!" World added.

"Facts! So, I get low and snatch out ana. I see a muthafucka in a hoodie running away and jump in a gray truck. I run out the hut, getting off ana. Knock the taillight out and shit, but the muthafucka got away!"

"Damn, I think I seen that truck right before you called," World enunciated.

"I'm sho you did! So, I got to the whip and see the hoe Kayla slumped, brains everywhere ana?"

"Not that baby!"

"Yeah, fam!" Face assured.

"Damn, how you feel about it?"

"Shid, to be one-K, that hoe needed her shit blowed off for how stank her pussy was," Face voiced with no empathy.

"Aww, maaan! You down bad for that one," World pronounced.

"Fuck all that. I think I know who did it," proclaimed Face.

"Talk to me."

"KoKo, bra!"

"Fuck no! Nigga, you trippin!" World stated.

Face pulled up the picture.

"Fuck is this?"

"This me in Orlando wit' Terrell at the Cheesecake Factory," Face explained.

"And?"

"And? Nigga, KoKo took this pic! She followed me to Orlando. On top of that, she told me to get rid of Terrell before she do."

"Oooooooweeee! KoKo done snapped!" World clowned, laughing. "All them niggaz you done flipped 'bout her; she done reversed that shit on yo' ass!" World continued to laugh.

"Shit ain't funny, fam!"

"Relax, bra. Trust me. If she wanted you dead, she woulda had you already. She spared you, fool. You done breed a straight demon! That's what a slice of the devil's pie get'cha!" World shook his head in a *I told you so* manner. "That's yo twin, nigga!" World added.

"Maan, fuck you, Blood!" Face spat, slightly irritated with his brother's antics. Face's phone rang. "Wassup, bae? I'm pulling up to the gate now," Face informed.

"Okay, I'm walkin' up now, daddy," Terrell responded calmly as if she'd been through this before.

"Aight."

Click! Face hung up.

"Look, I'ma bark at'chu tomorrow," Face told World, peacing him up.

"Aight! Let me know if you need help smokin' that hoe. I'm gone. 2-12 Damu," World pronounce.

"All the time," Face retorted, hopping out of the vehicle and meeting Terrell.

Chapter 20
Two-Hundred-Sixty-Nine

Face took a long, hot shower while Terrell gave her report to the officers. He had washed several times with men's Dove body wash, scrubbing thoroughly to remove any stench of Kayla from his body. Having Terrell report the car stolen, he knew his prints would come back conclusive but wasn't worried about it. He was Terrell's boyfriend, so his prints were expected to be present. When he made his way out of the shower, Terrell was completely relaxed, smoking a blunt. He climbed in bed and kissed her tenderly.

"Thank you, T," Face pronounced.

"No problem. You feel like tellin' me what happened now?" she implored, passing Face the blunt.

He took a pull before explaining the situation. "T, when I left you earlier, I did what I told you I was gone do. I pulled up on all the hoes and deaded it. I told'em that I was committing to you. The last one I told wanted me to get her some Rice Hut. I stepped in to order her food, then shots rang out," Face explained.

"Was it meant for you or her?" Terrell asked calmly, reaching for the blunt.

"I feel like it's a warning."

"From who?"

"Look, I'm not tryna get'chu involved, T-bae," Face expressed.

"Too late, Face. They found a bitch dead in my car. Who was it?" Her voice was stern.

"If I had to put my life on it, I'ma say KoKo," he asserted, hating to even mention KoKo's name.

Terrell nodded in a threatening manner. "You know I'm licensed to kill, right? My shit registered. If she come anywhere near me, I can blow that hoe down," Terrell asserted with a certain grimness.

Face shook his head. "No, I got it. Leave it alone."

Terrell's forehead creased in disbelief. "You still love this bitch?" Terrell implied, rising on her elbows.

"I'm not in love wit' her, but'chu know I got love for her."

Terrell kissed the back of her teeth.

"Just kuz I got love for her don't mean I won't pop her top. I'm different," he enunciated, placing a wet kiss on Terrell's soft sweet lips.

"Aight, but if she come anywhere near me, I'ma put that hoe down and won't do a day in jail," she warned.

"I hear you," Face assured when there was a knock at the door.

Terrell gave Face a dubious look. "You expecting somebody?" she implored, getting out of the bed.

"Nawl," Face stated.

"I'on have company. Nobody except my mama, and she gone call first," she added, grabbing her FN 509 to head to the door.

Face followed close behind with his pistol in clutch.

Terrell took a look out of the peephole. "The fuck?" she muttered then looked at Face. "You ordered food?" asked Terrell.

Face shook his head.

Terrell opened the door. "Wassup?" Terrell implored.

"Hi, ma'am, I have thirty boxes of pizzas for a Mr. Face," the young, geeky whiteboy pronounced.

"This shit wild," he said, shaking his head. "How much?" Face asked.

"Two hundred sixty-nine dollars and seventy cents, sir," the delivery man informed.

Face handed him three hundred. "Keep the change, homie. Just help me get 'em inside."

"No problem," said the delivery man, happy with his tip.

He helped Face secure the boxes in the kitchen, then thanked him for his generosity.

"You know that hoe did this, Face. That mean she know where I live, and I'on like that! Show me where this hoe live!" Terrell demanded.

"I got'chu; we gone lay on her tomorrow," Face promised, opening one of the pizza boxes.He noted a small note inside. Face read it and balled it up quickly before Terrell noticed.

She was busy stuffing her face. "Bae, I'm not gone lie, I was hungry as hell. I'ma thank that hoe right before I smoke her dumb ass," Terrell pronounced, devouring the pizza.

Face's mind was still on the note that read: "Enjoy your meal wit'cha new hoe! Then get rid if her like I told you! This is my last warning! You already know how I'm comin'. I LOVE YOU TILL DEATH!

Respectfully, You know who!"

Chapter 21
Let's Go Live

Terrell gasped as she lowered herself on Face's dick, stretching her with delectation. She rose slowly and descended aggressively, repeatedly until her rhythm became one aggressive motion bouncing on Face's dick in reverse cowgirl.

"Ffffuck, this dick so fuckin' good, baby." Terrell moaned, rubbing her clit while Face's hands caressed her back, sliding lower to cup her smooth and succulent ass cheeks.

"This yo dick! Sss, ffffuck yeah! That's it, ride that dick," Face encouraged through clenched teeth.

"Ooooohhh, ssssshit! I'm cum— sss— I'm cummin' on that dick, baby," she cried, switching her bounce to a grinding motion.

"Ssssshit!" Face yelled as he felt he wetness in his lap. He grabbed both of her hands then thrusted upwards; his dick head pressing against her G-Spot every stroke before hitting her cervix.

"Oh my God, yes! Fuck me, daddy! Ooowee!" She moaned in bliss.

"Ummhmmm!" Face taunted.

Unexpectedly, he rose from a sitting position then forced Terrell to turn around and lean on the bed with her hands still behind her back as if she were being detained. Face gave Terrell all that he had, using every muscle in his body to blow her back out. The arch in her back was extremely deep and her ass cheeks jiggled on impact.

"That's it! Take it! Take this dick! SSS…ummmhmm!" Face moaned as he came powerfully inside Terrell's box of happiness.

The warmth from Face's semen enticed Terrell to orgasm in tandem. She shook violently, waiting for the orgasm to subside, but Face intervened. He pulled out of her wet pussy, turned Terrell on her back, then latched on her clit with her legs spread eagle.

"Fuuck, fuck, fffffuck…daddy, what'chu doin' to me!"

Face kissed, licked, blew, and sucked until she creamed on his tongue and mouth. "Hmmm." Face moaned, swallowing all that her body dripped.

"Oooow, you eatin' this pussy!" she lamented.

Right when Terrell thought it was over, Face rose and slipped dick back in her and punished her for another five minutes until they both laid stretched from orgasms.

"Damn, baby! You gone have me round here killin' bout that dick too, you keep fuckin' me like that," Terrell clowned chasing her breath.

Face laughed it off, and moments later, his phone alerted that he had a message. He reached and grabbed his phone from the nightstand. It was a text from B3 at 10:40 a.m. Face opened the message.

"Nawl?"

"What, daddy?" Terrell implored.

Face handed her his phone.

"We ain't gone have to lay on her no time soon," Face pronounced.

It was a photo of KoKo's arrest.

"Possession of a firearm and possession of cocaine. It say that she was arrested on the outside of my gated community. That hoe was layin' on us, or layin' on me!" Terrell proclaimed, seething.Face listened intently.

"That hoe bond ain't nothin' but fifty-thousand! I'm finna post that hoe bond, then wait on her to walk and catch her ugly ass on Rock Road," Terrell enunciated, brimming with emotion.

"You ain't doin' none of that! That's out! I'm not finna lose you like that. Just take a breather and relax. It's gone work itself out, bae. Trust me," Face assured.

Terrell drew in a deep breath, then exhaled loudly. "Aight."

"Okay," Face added, kissing her tenderly.

***

Face pulled on Avenue S at his mother's house in his K5 with Terrell in the passenger seat. He had given her the money for a new car, but she hadn't decided on what she wanted yet. When the duo exited the vehicle, they were greeted by Sierra, World, Moses, and B3. A few other people lingered around who were associates of Moses and Sierra, who Face didn't know.

"Wassup, big bra?" Sierra greeted, hugging his neck.

"What up, lil nigga?" Face retorted.

"Don't what up me, nigga! I ain't seen you since you was s'pose to bring back that butter and garlic, nigga! I waited foreva on you," Sierra said, hitting Face playfully in the chest.

"My bad, I ran into a problem," Face pronounced, peacing World up. "Wass poppin'?" Face greeted World.

"Niggaz, like us," World replied.

"3, wass poppin', nigga? Moses, my nigga, wassup wit' it?" Face greeted, dapping Moses and B3 up in tandem.

"Hey, Terrell," Sierra spoke, hugging her.

"Wassup, Sierra," Terrell retorted, smiling.

"Come up here with me and have a drink," Sierra offered, pulling Terrell by the hand.

"Bae, I'm going up here to get a drink."

"Aight," Face pronounced.

"Okay, I view you! Went and got'cha baby back, huh? Better make sure KoKo don't find out," World clowned.

B3 chuckled.

"Y'all boyz wild," Moses added, smoking a blunt.

"Slide over here," World suggested, taking Face to the front yard where three cars were lined up back to back the long way—World's Mustang, B3's new Beema, and Moses' Trackhawk. When Face made it on the other side of the cars, he seen multiple rifles laid about on the ground. "Okay, sticked up on this good Friday evenin'!" Face asserted, smiling.

"You already know, we stay dressed to impress," World added—a Blood lingo meaning strapped with gunz.

"Who Beema?" Face asked.

"That's my bitch, mane. You like it?" B3 asked, gazing at it as if he'd just seen it for the first time.

"Most def!" Face pronounced.

"I heard 'bout KoKo," World stated, taking a shot from his bottle.

"I'on even want to politick 'bout that hoe," Face replied, shaking his head.

"Where mama at?"

"She went out to eat," World informed.

"Everythang good wit'cha?" Moses implored, passing Face a blunt.

"Yeah, I'm Gucci," Face assured.

***

"So you went and got'cha man back? You my sis nah," Sierra proclaimed.

"Let's go live," Sierra suggested, pulling her phone out.

"Yaaaahsss! I'm outside wit' my sis-n-law and the guys," Sierra stated, showing her surrounds in the background.

"It's givin' tranquility, freedom, and most definitely motion! Y'all see them steppaz back there! Yeah!" Sierra boasted.

***

After a few blunts and shots, Face and the guys were feelin' blissfully sedated. They bashed about sex, money, and murder while Terrell and Sierra watched them from the garage. While Sierra made conversation about something meaningless to Terrell, Terrell spotted a strange vehicle out of her periphery, creeping on her left. She dropped her shot glass and grabbed her pistol from her Celine's Bucket bag.

"Bae! Y'all get right!" Terrell yelled as the vehicle turned the corner with somebody hanging out of the passenger and back window.

BOC! BOC! BOC! BOC! BOC! BOC! BOC! Terrell let her gun blow, hitting the assailant in the back window in the head. World, Face, B3, and Moses all ducked behind the vehicles, then rose, firing multiple rounds from the ARP's, totaling the rental car that the assailants were in, forcing them to wreck out in a small man-made ditch.

Face, World, and B3 ran towards the vehicle while Moses went to check on Sierra and Terrell. BOC! BOC! BOC! BOC! BOC! BOC! BOC! BOC! BOC! BOC! BOC! BOC! BOC! BOC! BOC! The trio continued to fire upon the vehicle, Swiss cheesing everything inside. All windows had been shattered to pieces so the assailants-turned-victims could be seen clear as day, dead from multiple shots to the head and body. A sheer volume of blood and brains could be found all over the interior.

"I know them niggaz! Them Knight's people," Face exclaimed.

"Fuck 'em," World added.

"Come on, bae, we gotta go," Terrell asserted, pulling Face by the hand.

Face trotted back to his mother's yard.

"Y'all boyz go 'head. I got it," Moses stated.

Moses paid everybody's rent who lived in the neighborhood, so when the police came, they would say nothing or lie for him.

Face, World, and B3 hopped in their whips and fled the scene.

Chapter 22
You Done?

Face jumped on I-95 and headed north. He didn't want to be nowhere near Fort Pierce when their gruesome episode aired on the news.

"Bae, I gotta be real wit'chu," Terrell exclaimed.

"Wassup, ma?" Face retorted.

"The reason them niggaz came through like that is because yo' sister went live and showed y'all location. It ain't my place, but bae, if she knew y'all got smoke out here, she ain't have no bidness goin' live," Terrell voiced.

"Sierra know we got smoke. She was outta pocket, and she put our lives in danger. What if mama was outside?" Face spat.

"Luckily, I was on point. Yo' sister was talkin' my ear off, but I wasn't payin' her no attention. I knew it was smoke when I seen all them guns on the ground. When them niggaz bent that corner, I blew my shit and hit that nigga in the backseat," Terrell explained.

"I peeped that. Good lookin', bae. I love you for that."

Terrell smiled. "You know, I love you too," she retorted.

Face grabbed his phone and dialed out.

"Hello?"

"Wass poppin', nigga? This Face, nigga!"

"Ooh, shit, bloody, wass poppin'?" 210 Slick implored.

Slick was Face homie from Perry, Florida. They had did a prison bid together and promised to link up on the outside.

"Look, bra, I'm on the road headed to you. I done performed and need to lay low for a few days," Face enunciated.

"Yeah, bih, you already know! Bring ya ass on, nigga! On that other tip, you already know how I'm rockin'. I'll slide down there, knock some shit off, and get back on the road, bih," Slick asserted anxiously.

"I know, Bloody. We'll bark when I touchdown," Face assured.

"Already! I been tellin' these niggaz 'bout'cha down here! I'm sending you the addy nah. I'ma view you when you get here. Love, Damu," Slick exclaimed.

"2-12, Damu," Face retorted. Click!

***

"Wassup, brodi?" Sierra answered.

"What it look like?" Face questioned casually.

"We good. Moses had somebody clean up real good. They had this bitch taped off and shit, but ain't nobody said nothin'," she informed.

"Fasho. Where World and 3?"

"World ducked off; he took 3 wit' him," Sierra added.

"You know this shit on you, right?"

"What'chu mean?" Sierra implored, confused.

"I viewed you went live! You gave up our exact location! It's real smoke out here, sis. You know better than that!" Face snapped.

"Don't do that! Them niggaz was gone come regardless! Y'all knew what y'all doin' out here!" Sierra retorted, trying to defend her fuck-up.

"Exactly! We know how we movin'; that's why we don't go fuckin' live!"

Sierra kissed the back of her teeth. "You trippin'!" Sierra added.

"Yeah, I know it!" Face barked.

Click! Face hung up the phone on Sierra, not wanting to argue. Arguing was not something Face knew how to do. All he knew was action.

***

World was driving a golf cart with B3 on the side of him, headed to his Uncle Mott's mansion to grab the dirt bikes when his phone rang.

"Wass poppin', big bra?" World answered.

"You already know, that five! Wassup though, where you at, bih?" Face implored.

"I'm on the Indian reservation at Mya house, but I'm headed to Uncle Mott's to grab the bikes. Me and B3."

"Fasho. I'm headed to the Panhandle. Remember I let'chu hear my nigga, 210 Slick from Perry?"

"Oh, yeah! Fool be slidin'. What about him?"

"I'm headed to Perry, Florida to kick it wit' 'em for a few days. Let shit die down a lil piece," Face proclaimed.

"Same shit. That's why I'm out here fuckin' with these bikes. Aye, Terrell still wit'chu?" World asked.

"Yeah, she wit' me. Wassup?"

"Man, tell her she did that! That's my sis-n-law! Sis a kold gangsta fa real!" World exclaimed.

"She can hear you," Face assured.

"Hey, bro! I was just doin' what needed to be done," Terrell pronounced.

"Already!" World added.

"We gone vibe later, bloody," Face interjected.

"2-12."

"2-12, Damu," Face replied. Click!

***

116

Face had stopped at a rest spot to grab some cigars and Red Stripe beers. He swapped with Terrell and let her drive while he blew ZaZa and gathered his thoughts.

"I love you, daddy," Terrell voiced, interrupting Face's thoughts.

He took in what she had just disclosed to him and processed it before replying. "I love you too," Face retorted.

Terrell smiled from ear to ear. "You sure?"

"Positive!" He assured, hitting the blunt and passing it to her.

"You just gave life more meaning. Thank you," Terrell expressed, tearing up.

Face leaned over and licked a tear that was cascading down her cheek, then kissed where the tear once was.

"The feelin' is mutual," Face replied, with his phone ringing afterwards.

He seen that it was his cousin Chere.

"Wassup, fam?" Face answered.

"Kuz, wassup? I'm callin' to check on you," Chere exclaimed.

"Everythang Gucci over here. Appreciate'chu hittin' me up. How you been?"

"You already know! I'm always good."

"Already!"

"Fam, don't be mad at me," Chere stated.

"'Bout what?" Face questioned, confused.

"Wassup, Face?" another voice chimed in that Face knew by sound.

"Tsss... fam, why you got this slimey ass hoe on my line?" Face barked, causing Terrell to look over at him.

He swiped his hand at the air as a gesture to let her know not to worry.

"Just hear her out, Kuz," Chere begged.

"Maaaan, how? What'chu want!" implored Face.

"What I want is for you to stop actin' like you don't love me no moe! You outta all people should know how I'm comin' 'bout'chu!" KoKo threatened.

"Hoe, you done?" Face snapped.

"Really, Face?" KoKo inquired.

"Hoe, drank bleach!"

Click! Face hung up on them both.

"You alright?" Terrell asked, reaching over to rub Face's chest.

"I'm wit'chu, so fuck yeah! I'm great!"

Terrell smiled happily. "You know what to say to get this pussy wet, don't'chu?" she implied, rubbing between his thighs.

"This shit automatic," Face clowned, then hit his blunt.

Chapter 23
Stupid Ass Boy!

World had hopped on a Yamaha YZ 250 while B3 chose the Yamaha YZ 450. It was a dying afternoon, and the sun was quite low when they made it four miles out into the woods where a large hut had been built out of wood and palm leaves. It appeared to be two occupants occupying the hut when World and B3 pulled up.

"Sssss, ooow, ffffuck yeah! Ssss…yes! Ummhmm… ffffuck!" a woman moaned as she rode the dick of a dread-headed man under the hut.

He appeared to be startled by World and B3's presence and told his partner such. She turned and observed who had interrupted their freak off.

"Tammy T?" World called out.

Tammy squinted and focused in on the intruders. "World?"

"Yeah, this me!"

"Damn, wassup, Kuz?" Tammy implored excitedly.

Tammy T and World were related by marriage.

"You already know, out'chere on this bike life. I'ma flex though. I ain't mean to fuck up ya groove," World exclaimed.

"Nawl, Kuz, you straight! Don't leave! You got some weed?" Tammy asked, pulling her panties back up under her sundress.

"You know it! B3, twist up," World insisted.

"Already," B3 replied.

119

"Who that, Kuz?" Tammy asked, approaching the two.

"This my nigga, B3; this my kuzin, Tammy T."

"Nice to meet'chu," B3 spoke.

"You too," Tammy replied.

"Aye, why the fuck you askin' 'bout that nigga for? You see me right here, hoe! Yo' so damn disrespectful!" the dread head snapped.

"Nigga, this my people," Tammy fired back.

"Hoe, I'on give no fucks 'bout'cha people," he continued.

"Fam, who this clown ass nigga is?" World questioned.

"That's just Arkbar, the tattoo man," she brushed off.

"Arkbar," World mumbled to himself as he ran the name through his mental database. "Oh, Arkbar," World muttered again as he remembered exactly who he was. "Kuz, you love this nigga?" World implied.

"Fuck no! I just met 'em a week ago at the casino," Tammy T pronounced, grabbing the blunt from B3.

World hopped off the bike and leaned it on its stand. "Arkbar, wass poppin', my boy?" World implored, walking towards him, closing the space between them.

B3 climbed off of the four-wheeler and inched his way toward the duo.

"Ain't shit poppin' but his hoe big ass pussy! I'll appreciate it if you niggaz leave, so she can get back to it!" Arkbar spat.

Tammy T laughed and shook her head. "Whateva, lil dick ass nigga," she shot back.

"You don't remember me?" World asked.

"I mean, you look familiar, but who gives a fuck, really? I'm tryin' to get my dick wet, and you lil niggaz is in the way," Arkbar pronounced, standing up.

"You did all my tattoos on my stomach," World proclaimed, lifting his shirt.

Arkbar kissed the back of his teeth. "Nigga, how the fuck you expect me to see out here wit' no—"

Boc! Boc! B3 hit Arkbar in the side of his head, dropping him odiously.

Boc! Boc! Boc! World hit him three more times on general principle.

"Stupid ass boy," World stated, tucking his pistol.

"Damn, Kuz. I thought you was gone beat his ass or some shit! Y'all done left his ass stankin'! Lil dick ass," she added.

"I'on know, fam, you was moaning pretty good when we pulled up," World clowned.

"Boy, bye! I do that wit' any size. Fuck all that though. It'a a pond a lil further out that shit like quicksand. They'll neva find his lil dick ass back there," Tammy stated, lighting a cigarette.

"Shid, B3, let's lay 'em across the four-wheeler and dump 'em in there," World suggested.

"Say no moe, mane," B3 retorted.

"Let's do it," World added, helping B3 lay the body across the four-wheeler.

Disrespecting Tammy T was not the only reason for Arkbar's death. World and B3 both knew that Face had killed Arkbar's brother Miami in their tattoo shop. After everything that's been happening, they weren't leaving him room to retaliate. He had to go.

***

Face and Terrell had been in Perry for six days hanging out with the greatest. Slick had taken them to a club called "THE MOON," but they mainly hung out in the trap house most of the time. "Bitch, how you feelin'?" Slick asked Face fifteen minutes after giving him an e-pill.

"Bitch, I'm jiggin'," Face retorted in a molly tone, feeling galvanized.

"Yeah, bitch, I told you! Deez them 2005 X-pillz! Straight gas!" Slick boasted.

"Look, man, hit whoever you gotta hit up. I need ten thousand pillz to take back to my city," Face proclaimed, licking his lips and wiping his face.

"Ten thousand? Shid… I'll give 'em to you for fifty cent apiece," Slick assured.

"I ball that," Face stated, going in his pocket and counting out the money for the pillz.

When Face handed Slick the money, he noted how Slick just held the money in his hand and fell into deep thought.

"What'chu thinkin' 'bout, Bloody?" questioned Face, lighting a cigarette.

"Tonight, why, wassup?"

"You feel like makin' another five thousand pillz?" Slick proposed.

"Run it," Face accepted.

One of Slick's homies walked out of the house that they were trapping in and approached. "Aye, Slick, my kracka finna swang through for ten blues. Gone catch 'em. I'm out. I'm finna go to this lil bitch house, fuck wit'cha later," Chub pronounced.

"Aight, bra," Slick retorted.

"Aight, Face, bra, nice meetin' you," Chub asserted, dapping Face up before leaving.

"Already," Face replied.

"Damn, Tia blowin' up my phone," Slick stated, looking at his phone.

"Terrell blowin' my shit, too. Let me view what'chu talkin' 'bout wit' deez pillz," Face pronounced.

"Shid… let's roll."

***

Face walked through a projects called "The Section" and surveyed its way of life. It was county and a bit slow, but the women were so beautiful and well built. He spotted one high-yellow, thicker than grits, leaning in the window of a

Chevy Caprice talking to a well-known drug dealer. "Damn, that bitch fine," Face muttered from a distance. "Fuck it," he said out loud to himself as he approached her fervently.

She had a forty-inch weave hanging right to the bottom of her thick, soft-looking ass cheeks. Face disrespectfully grabbed a handful of her weave and pulled her away from the window.

Boc! Boc! Boc! Boc! Face pointed his pistol directly in the man's face and hit him four times, killing him instantly. The beautiful woman didn't scream but took off running the moment Face let her hair go. Face trotted through some apartments and hopped in a getaway car that Slick was waiting in. Slick pulled off smooth and headed back to the spot.

"You got 'em, Bloody?" Slick asked eagerly.

Face gave him a knowing look.

"Fuck you think? I'ma dog," Face boasted.

Chapter 24
Run Ya Mouth

After laying low for a week, Face, World, and B3 hit club Elks, stepping in their best. Face had given B3 and World a thousand pillz apiece, so their presence in the club was strictly business. The whole city had heard what happened on Avenue S, so all eyes were glued to the trio. All three men had a bottle of Remy in hand while doing a walk-through, grilling friendly and opposition. The sounds of Albee Al's "Don't Compare Me" serenaded the atmosphere and intensified the x-pills that they'd popped.

Face gritted his teeth and stopped in front of a group of niggaz who he knew were related to Knight. He toyed with his 800-gram Cuban necklace, then held his wrist out, turning it back and forth so that the Baquet bracelet and Cuban diamonds diddly danced in their faces. "Wass poppin', Low?" Face implored, while World was bouncing up and down demonically, daringly.

"What up, nigga?" Low replied in a non-threatening manner.

"Go replace them dead ass flowers on ya nigga grave!" Face stated, putting the fear of God in all who heard him. "Y'all be screamin' that nigga name like he was legendary; that fuck nigga was a nobody! Y'all know, he mentioned my name before he died! He died a rat!" Face yelled, still playing with his jewels.

"Yeah! Wass poppin'? Wassup?" World taunted.

B3 just stood on go, bobbing his head to the music.

"You niggaz know wassup!" Face pronounced, using his middle finger, index, and thumb to shape his hand into a pistol form.

No one combated his remark.

"Blood Gang, nigga!" Face barked before mobbing off.

"Suwooop!" World added, following close behind Face, while B3 secured the front.Face found a spot in the cut and posted up. Moments later, the pill heads started making their way to the cut they were in for purchasing purposes.

"What'chu need, shawdy?" B3 asked a petite, dark, slim beauty.

"TSSSS…!" she replied, putting her hand in B3's face as a gesture of dismissal.

"Umm! Face, wassup?" Quanda implored aggressively, with her left hand on her hip and her right hand still in B3's face.

"First off! Get'cha hand out my nigga face before I slap the shit out'cha!" Face snapped.

Quanda removed her hand from B3's face. "So, you really gone put hands on me 'bout this nigga?"

"Bitch! What the fuck you want?" Face retorted, looking her up and down with disdain.

An expression of hurt plastered across Quanda's face. "I just wanna talk, Face," she pleaded.

"Maaan, hoe, get the fuck on!"

"Face!" she cried, attempting to touch him.

He smacked her hand away. "You knew exactly what'chu was doin' when you posted that picture of us on Facebook! You knew that hoe was gone go stupid and put the law on me! Bitch, leave!" Face demanded, mushing Quanda in her face.

"Face, please! I was just hurt! Let me make it—!"

Smack! A woman came from out of nowhere, attacking Quanda like an untamed guerrilla, pummeling her to the floor. World and B3 reached for their weapons but relaxed when they noted it was just two women.

"Yeah, bitch! I told ju, hoe! Bitch! Bitch! Hoe! That's my shit, bitch!" KoKo yelled, while beating the blood from Quanda's face.

Seconds later, a BBW jumped in on the onslaught, kicking and stomping Quanda's ribs.

"Ummhmm! Bitch! Beat that hoe, KoKo!" Chere yelled, while kicking Quanda repeatedly.

"Kuz, what the fuck?" Face implored dubiously.

Before Chere could explain, one of Quanda's brothers hit Chere in the jaw with a weak hook. Out of pure instinct, Face threw a straight right jab, dropping him instantly. World and B3's assistance was automatic. They stomped Quanda's cousin out until security showed up.

"Face, come on, fam, y'all gotta go!" Big Rude exclaimed as he and his posse grabbed Quanda and her brother to be removed from the club.

"Let's roll," Face told his steppaz.

Once outside, World and B3 stalked Quanda's brother.

"Yeah boy, I gotta have you!" World threatened.

"Fam, what'chu doin' with this hoe?" Face asked Chere.

"Shid, Kuz, you know I fuck wit' KoKo. I just bonded her out today. We just came out tonight to hang, but when KoKo seen girl all in yo' face, she snapped."

"Face, let me talk to you for a minute. All I need is a minute," KoKo pronounced.

"Fuck no!" Face retorted, heading to his vehicle.

"Kuz, just give her a minute," Chere pleaded.

"Just hear the hoe out real quick so we can go," World added, to Face's surprise.

Face gave World a questionable look.

"Me and B3 gone be over here watchin' shit; you good," World assured.

"Maaan, run yo mouth," Face barked, folding his arms across his chest.

KoKo approached calmly, only inches away from Face's face. He silently admired her glowing skin and jail weight that put thickness in all the right spots.

"Face, I love you," she started off.

"Bullshit!" he debated.

KoKo shook her head from left to right.

"Face, the night my brother died, I was in my mama' house in the back room. You don't think I seen you and B3 come outta Lexus' apartment, creeping by my window wit' blue rags on y'all face? Nigga, if I didn't love you, I woulda been lined you and B3 up. Then you had the nerve to call me the next day and console me. You picked me up and fuck the shit outta me after killin' my brother. You different! But that's why I love you, nigga."

"I'on know what'chu talkin' bout," Face lied.

"You know me better than that. Listen, movin' forward, don't ask me 'bout no Lexus, that hoe Kayla, or nobody! After that shit wit' my brother, I got the right to brang a move on whoever the fuck I want to," KoKo sneered through clenched teeth.

Unbeknownst to her, she was turning Face on. He had to catch himself.

"Look, I hear all that shit, but you lied about having my son. That shit hit different," Face admitted.

KoKo scurried to Chere's car and came back.

"Here," KoKo said, handing Face a birth certificate and social security card that read FAYZON KING.

He examined it, then looked up at KoKo.

"So, why would Cee Cee lie on the baby?" he implored.

"I'on know, Face. Maybe she wanted you," KoKo implied.

"Did you—"

"No, I didn't kill my sister, Face. They lying about someone taking the baby. I picked Fayzon up that mornin' way before they found her," KoKo lied.

"So, where he at now?"

"At Chere apartment wit' a babysitter."

Face nodded his head. "Aight. I wanna view him tomorrow," Face stated.

"No problem, daddy," KoKo replied seductively.

***

Smack! Smack! Smack! Smack! Smack! Smack! The sounds of KoKo's ass cheeks smacking against Face's thighs repetitiously blared throughout the room at the Quality Inn.

"Ooooww, I feel you, daddy!" KoKo cried while bouncing wildly on Face's dick.

"Ffffffuck!" Face yelled as the sight of KoKo's thick ass cheeks bounced and jiggled with every thrust.

KoKo leaned forward and sucked Face's nipple while still bouncing on his dick. She knew that this technique would make Face cum within seconds and went for the gusto.

"Ooohh, ssshit!" he moaned as the warmth from her mouth on his nipple and the warmth from her pussy on his dick hit simultaneously, making him grow longer and as hard as obsidian.

"Sssss, ooow, daddy...you hard! Why you so hard, daddy?"

"You know this pussy good, bitch!" Face stated through clenched teeth.

He gripped both of her ass cheeks and lifted her up and down, slamming all his dick in and out of her truculently.

"Whoooo, daddy! I feel you! Sssss...ssshit! Pussy skeetin', daddy," KoKo wailed as she came all over Face's dick and cried tears of joy.

"Damn, this pussy wet," Face added while the sounds of her wetness smacked loudly throughout the room.

"This yo' pussy, daddy," she assured, clamping her pussy walls around his dick.

"Ooooow, I'm finna nut in this pussy!" Face yelled.

KoKo hopped off Face's dick and stuck it deep in her warm throat. She gagged but kept bobbing her head up and down rapidly, catching and swallowing every drop of Face's semen."Mmmmm," KoKo moaned, loving the taste and texture.

Face shook irrepressibly while gripping the sheets. Knowing that the head of his dick was most sensitive after an orgasm, she focused on it and applied pressure.

"Ssss, ffffuck! Aight! That's enough," Face yelled, prying KoKo's mouth from his dick.

"You still can't handle this mouth," KoKo boasted, placing kisses up Face's thigh to his stomach and chest until she was snuggled up under him, laying her head on his chest.

"I miss you, daddy," KoKo voiced, rubbing on Face's chest.

"Missed you too," Face retorted, gazing at the roof.

"So, what we doin'?" KoKo implored.

"I wanna view my son."

"Okay, daddy. You'll see him today," she promised.

Seconds later, Face's phone rang. He grabbed it and saw that it was Terrell calling. "Fuck," he mumbled.

"Wassup, daddy?" KoKo questioned.

"Well, link up later. I gotta go," he enunciated, getting up to get dressed.

"Here we go," KoKo cried.

Chapter 25
Paper Money

"Face, where the hell you at?" Terrell asked as calm as she could.

"I just got back in town. I had to make a play on some jiggz," Face lied referring to X-pillz.

"Where you at right now?"

"Pullin' in my mama's driveway as we speak," Face exclaimed really pulling into his mother's driveway where World was posted having a drink.

"What happened last night?" she implored.

From Face's experience with women, he knew that most of the time when a woman asked you something it's because she already knows and wants to see if you lie about it.

"What'chu mean?" Face replied trying to see what she knew.

"In the club? What happened?"

"Me and the guys got into a lil scuffle, nothin' major," Face explained.

"Over KoKo?" Terrell interjected smoothly.

"Fuck no! She was in there, but we ain't talk. What had happen was...a female was all in my face and while I'm tellin' her to leave me alone, KoKo came from out of nowhere and put hands on her. My cousin Chere was with her, and they jumped the girl. A nigga who must have been the girl's brother hit my cousin Chere, and we got right on his ass. So, fuck no, it wasn't bout no KoKo. It was bout my people."

"Okay. When I'ma see you?" she asked in a molly tone.

"I'ma handle a lil bidness, then we gone link," Face assured.

"That's fine," Terrell proclaimed her tone still even.

"You good?"

"As long as you okay…I'm wonderful. I love you, Face."

"Love you too, T."

"Later," Click!

Face hopped out of the K5 and approached World.

"Top of the top!" World greeted bumping B's with Face.

"Top of the 5th," Face replied.

World handed Face the bottle.

"What'chu did up there in that Kountry ass spot?" implored World.

"Don't sleep on Perry! It's plenty of money, and thick shit up there."

"Nigga, you had Terrell wit'chu! She ain't goin'! Ain't no way!" World clowned.

"I'on fuck off. I picked up some work and put some work in before I got in the wind," Face pronounced taking a shot of the Don Julio.

"This shit wild," World stated.

"Wassup?"

"Me, and 3 had to put a nigga down on the reservation," World asserted.

"Nawl!"

"Yeah…deep off in the woods. You won't believe who!" World added with a sinister smirk on his face.

"Run ya mouth," Face interjected quickly.

"Arkbar," World informed grabbing his bottle form Face grasp.

"For what?"

"Shid, why not? You flipped his brother. I just killed any opportunity of retaliation. Plus, the nigga was talkin' real spicy to fam."

"Who?"

131

"Tammy T!"

"The fuck she doin' wit' Arkbar in the woods?" Face asked.

"We pulled up on them fuckin' and shit. You shoulda viewed how B3 hit that nigga in his head, Boy sprayed his brains all over me and shit. I had to hit the fool three moe times ana?"

"I respect. My nigga B3 been performing lately, huh?" Face proclaimed smiling.

"Yeah, yeah, boy turnt! Wassup wit'chu and KoKo. She ain't try to bontact you after that shit in the Elks?" World questioned.

"Nawl. I ain't heard from her," Face lied.

World shook his head up and down.

"You moved them pillz yet?" Face questioned changing the conversation.

"Oh yeah! I'm app you the money," World promised.

"App me the money? Nigga, pay me in paper money! You trippin', Blood?"

"Maan, I'm app it to ya nigga!" World retorted.

Face's phone rang.

"Paper money!" Face barked then answered his phone.

"Wass poppin?"

"Niggas like us!" Assata replied.

"All the time! What's the word?"

"I need you to pick somethin' up for me," said Assata.

"Anything for the Queen. Send me the addy,"

Seconds later Face's phone alerted.

"Got it."

"Aight. Ask for Yolonda. She gone give you a package and just bring it to me," Assata instructed.

"I'm on it," Face assured.

"2-12 Damu!"

"2-12, Bloody!" Face replied. Click!

"Look I gotta handle a lil bidness. I'on want no electric money. Get that paper money up, pronto lil nigga!" Face stated walking off and jumping in his whip.

"Whatever nigga!" World retorted.

***

When Face pulled into the location he see that it was a plaza of some sort off of US 1Highway. Parking his car and hopping out, he approached the building, located the suite, and pressed the buzzer. There was a sign that read "YOLONDA'S TAXES on the door. Moments later the door popped open.

"Yes, can I help you?" an older woman asked with the door cracked.

"Yeah, I'm lookin' for Yolonda. I'm here for Assata," Face answered.

"Oh, okay. Come on in honey," Yolonda invited opening the door for Face.

When he entered Face noted all type of merchandise from T-shirts, bottled water, cupcakes, to machinery he never seen before.

"Would you like a drink or refreshment?"

"No, thank you. Just pulled up for the package," Face stated.

"Okay, follow me back here."

Yolonda lead Face to a back room where all types of identifications were laid about.

"Here," Yolonda said handing Face a manila envelope.

"Appreciate it," Face replied grabbing the package and turning to leave.

"Wait, hold on! You sho you don't need anything?"

"Just look at this real quick. I just did these," Yolonda mentioned walking over to a table.

Face kissed the back of his teeth silently and approached the table.

"See," she said sliding the identifications in front of Face.

Examining the identification, Face heartrate increased while all kind of nefarious thoughts plagued his mind. Clear as day a birth certificate and social security card read: "FAZON KING."

Chapter 26
You Broke My Heart

"She ain't give you no problems, did she, Blood?" Assata pried, grabbing the package from Face.

"Nawl, she was vibrant. Vibrant and informative," Face muttered, looking off to the side.

"I appreciate'chu, Bloody," Assata asserted, standing parrot-toed.

"No pressure," Face shot back.

"You feel like standin' up in something?" Assata implored, opening her robe before having a seat with her legs stretched open. "I'on want'chu to feel like I beat'chu out'cha head. Push up," Assata offered.

Damn this muthafucka gorgeous! Face thought, removing his shirt while closing the space between them.

The moment Face's lips made contact with Assata's, *his* phone rang.

"Hold up," she stated, placing her hand on Face's six-pack and answering the phone.

"Wass poppin'?"

"You gotta visitor, Queen," Shooter informed.

"Who?"

"Him," Shooter answered.

"Aight."

Click! Assata hung up.

"You gotta go, we'll bark later," Assata proclaimed, standing to close her robe.

"Overstood," Face assured, walking to the front door. "I'll have that baby love for you tomorrow," Face added, referring to money.

"2-12."

"All the time," Face retorted before walking out the door.

Face spotted lil Fif God and Shooter posted at the bottom of the steps keeping the visitor at bay.

"Who the fuck is this nigga?" asked the visitor with a screw face.

Face made his way past the lil homies and stepped in front of the visitor.

"If you gotta ask that, you can't be from the city," Face pronounced with a poise that exuded masculinity.

"Nigga, I'on give no fucks about'chu!"

"Wass poppin', bitch-ass nigga?" Face implored calmly, snatching his pistol out at the same time as his opposition.

They both held pistols pointed at each other's head.

"Squeeze, nigga!"

"Wheneva you ready," Face replied.

"G.I.... Face! Both of y'all stand the fuck down!" Assata ordered, leaning on the rail.

G.I. was the father of Assata's child.

"Fuck all that!" G.I. snapped.

Lil Fif God and Shooter pointed their weapons at Face and G.I.

"Watch yo' fuckin' mouth!" Shooter warned.

"The Queen has spoken! Put'em down," lil Fif warned.

Face tucked his pistol.

"View you later, sweet thang," Face clowned, blowing a kiss at G.I. before walking off.

"Yeah, aight nigga," G.I. countered, tucking his gun.

Face jumped in his whip and left the scene.

"Who the fuck was that?" G.I. snapped, looking up at Assata, attempting to walk up the steps.

"Hold up, playboy!" Shooter asserted, his pistol pointed at G.I.

"G.I., get the fuck from 'round here," Assata stated before walking back inside.

"Assata!" he yelled.

"You heard her! Get the fuck on, nigga!" Shooter snapped.

G.I. shook his head.

"Yeah, aight!"

***

Face took his car and swapped it out with Terrell's new Lexus E5 350. It was matte black with red leather interior and five-percent tint. He kissed her, left some money, and told her that he would be back later. Terrell didn't protest, and that was a trait that Face loved about her.

Heading back in the hood, Face dialed World's number only to get sent to voicemail. He tried three more times then said, *fuck it.*

"This nigga here, man!" Face yelled, seething. "I told this nigga I need my fuckin' money!"

His phone rang.

"Yeah!"

"Hey bro," Sierra stated, hoping Face didn't hang up on her.

Face exhaled loudly.

"Wassup, man?" Face retorted, irritated.

"I won't take up too much of yo' time. Just wanted to tell you I'm sorry for dropping the location on live, and that I love you," Sierra enunciated.

A few moments of silence tickled by before Face replied.

"Don't trip, you good, sis. We was lookin' for them niggaz anyway. I love you too, lil nigga."

Sierra laughed, happily elated to be speaking to her brother again.

"Look, I been tryin' to find World, but the nigga ain't pickin' up," Face said, grabbing an X-pill and popping it in his mouth.

Instead of swallowing it, he chewed it, then washed it down with a shot of Don Julio.

"He prolly bizzy gettin' his house situated. You know he just gotta spot off of 29th Street and G."

"Oh yeah? Which one?" Face implored, heading towards 29th Street.

"Next door to Randy them people," she retorted.

"Aight, look sis, I'm finna bust a move. I'ma fuck with'chu later," he promised, making a right on 29th and Avenue G.

"Okay, love you bro," Sierra expressed.

"Love you too, nigga."

Click! Face hung up the phone and pulled in the yard that was supposed to be World's. He took another shot before hopping out and approaching the door. Instead of knocking, Face turned the knob and opened it. He entered, inhaling and exhaling blissfully from the pill, gritting his teeth.

"Ffffuck," he muttered, rubbing his hand across his face and licking his lips.

There was no one in the living room, so Face made a left and proceeded down the hallway.

"Hhhaaa! Ssshit! Sss, oooow, right there! Sss, right there! Oooow, I'm nuttin', nigga, ssshit..." a voice moaned in the first room on the right.

When Face tiptoed to the door, he found that it was cracked. He pushed it open slowly and couldn't believe what was unfolding before him.

Clap! Clap! Clap! Clap! Clap! Clap! Face stood in the doorway in disbelief while watching his main man clap KoKo's cheeks from behind. Neither one of them heard Face enter the room, his pistol in hand. Their temerity stirred a torrid typhoon deep within Face's soul. A single tear cascaded down the right side of his face as he inched closer.

"Whoooo, daddy!" KoKo yelled.

She turned her head to the left to look at B3 while biting her bottom lip and spotted Face standing there. Her heart dropped to her pussy.

"Aaaah!" she yelled, leaping forward off of B3's dick and crawling into a corner of the room.

"What the hell wrong, mane?" B3 implored.

KoKo pointed behind him. When B3 turned around, Face placed the barrel of his FN to his forehead.

"Come on, mane! Let me explain, mane!" B3 pleaded with his hands up.

"You broke my heart," Face whispered and squeezed a shot off.

A neat red hole drilled in his skull, dropping and killing him instantly.

"Face, wait!" KoKo cried, her hands and arms reached out.

"Brang yo' ass here," Face demanded calmly, motioning with his pistol.

"Face, listen! He told me he was gone kill me if I didn't fuck him. I swear to God on my dead sister! He raped me! You know out of all people, I would never fuck B3!" she lied, producing fake tears.

"Sssshh. I know, bae. I believe you."

Face motioned for her to come closer, and she did, crawling slowly with a studious expression. When she reached the edge of the bed, Face pulled his dick out.

"You know what to do," he stated evenly, with an unreadable expression on his face.

The moment she attempted to put her mouth on his dick, Face grabbed her by the throat and jammed the barrel in her mouth.

"Aaahhgg!" KoKo gagged and vomited all over Face's pants.

"Stupid-ass bitch! You can't even help it! Just a slut by nature!" he snapped.

"Face!" KoKo managed to say in between coughing and catching her breath.

Crack! Face whacked her across the head with his pistol, putting her to sleep instantly. He headed out front and moved Terrell's car around back, leaving the trunk open. Once back inside, Face heard a strange noise coming from the room on the left. Pistol in hand, he pushed the door open and was deeply astounded to find the same baby that Cee Cee had in Wal-Mart strapped in a car seat playing with a baby rattle. Face shook his head in disgust.

"This hoe vicious," Face muttered, tucking his gun, then grabbing the baby.

He strapped the baby in the passenger's seat then went back for KoKo. She was still unconscious when he entered the room. Before grabbing her, he went through B3's pockets and confiscated seven thousand. He shook his head, disappointed.

"Damn, you played fool," he mumbled, stepping over B3 to grab KoKo.

Face grabbed her and loaded her in the trunk.

Chapter 27
No Body, No Case

"Bra, where you at?" World implored anxiously.

"I'm headin' back in town; I'm leavin' Gifford," Face lied. "Why, wassup?" he added.

"Maan, I just found the nigga B3 dead in my shit!"

"Stop playin', fam!" Face replied.

"Dead ass, bra! I left him there to go handle some bidness. I pull back up and find the nigga dead in my shit! Fuck, man! The fuck I'ma tell these crakaz?" World vented.

"Shid, tell'em the truth. Tell'em you found 'em like that. I'll be there in a few. Fuck! Not my nigga, man!" Face performed.

Click! Face hung the phone up and fell into deep thought while heading to the waterfall on 13th Street behind Francis K. Sweet Elementary School. The waterfall was a part of Taylor's Creek. At a certain time of day, the levy was lowered to let the water flow out into the ocean.

Face was thinking: *What if it was my brother instead of B3 fuckin' KoKo? Would I have killed him?* The thought alone sent chills throughout his body.

Bing! Face's Cash App alerted him. When he checked it, he seen that World had sent him his money.

"Damn," Face whispered. "This nigga gotta body layin' in his house and still made time to send me my money?" he thought, pulling next to the waterfall.

He hopped out, opened the trunk, and found KoKo conscious and surprisingly calm.

"Face, I love you," she pronounced in a molly tone.

"Bitch, get the fuck out the trunk!" Face demanded, motioning with his pistol.

KoKo did as she was told.

"Before you do this, let me talk to you," she tried to reason.

"Get the baby outta the front seat," he ordered through clenched teeth.

KoKo complied.

"Get the fuck over there!" he pointed at the railing.

"So, what'chu gone do? You gone kill me and yo' baby?" KoKo implored, tears falling from her eyes.

Face narrowed his eyes and shook his head in disgust.

"I went and seen Yolonda," Face stated, going in his pocket and pulling out his fake copies of Fayzon's birth certificate and social security card. "Bitch, that ain't my baby hoe!" Face yelled, placing the barrel in the middle of her forehead.

KoKo's eyes turned demonic at the sound of Yolonda's name.

"That bitch told you that?" KoKo questioned.

"Maaan, fuck all that! You killed yo' own sister?"

KoKo didn't blink as she held the sleeping baby.

"You killed Lexus?"

"Nigga, you killed my brother!" KoKo snapped. "You tryna act like you so fuckin' innocent, nigga. You dun killed muthafuckas too! You done fucked around and did me bad too, nigga. We even! So nigga, get that gun the fuck out my face and let's go home! And I'on give a fuck what Yolonda said — nigga, this yo' baby! We been trying to have a baby for a whole year, nigga. Yo' sperm count low! Yo' shit ain't swimming, so I went and got us a baby! Nigga, this is yo' fuckin' son!" KoKo barked, spit lodged in the corners of her mouth.

"Bitch, fuck you and that baby, you retarded-ass bitch!"

"Fuck me and yo' baby, huh? Yeah, aight," she retorted, throwing the baby over the railing into the deep murky water.

"What now?" she inquired, her arms outstretched.

Boc! Boc! Face hit KoKo twice in the chest, causing her to spin and drop face-first in the dirt.

He stood over her. *Boc!* He put one more in the back of her head, then hopped in his whip and vanished.

***

When Face pulled into World's yard, the ambulance was pulling away with B3's lifeless body in it while World stood on the porch in bewilderment. Face parked and hopped out to greet his brother.

"Wassup lil bra, you good?" Face implored, peacing World up.

"Hell nawl," World replied, wiping his hand across his face. "Somebody killed my nigga! I liked B3, man; he was solid. Nah, I gotta go down here to the police station for questioning and shit," World pronounced.

Face shook his head with guilt.

"My bad, my nigga," Face apologized.

"Yo' bad for what?" World retorted, confused.

Face exhaled deeply.

"Look fam, I was blowin' yo' phone up tryna collect that lil money you owe me, but'chu wasn't pickin' up," Face asserted.

"My shit was dead," World added.

"Yeah... anyway, sis called me and ended up tellin' me you gotta new spot. I pull up, and fall in ya spot, my nigga, and hear somebody clappin' cheeks the greatest. I push the door open and view B3 fuckin' KoKo in yo' shit," Face explained.

"Nawl?" World added.

***

"On Blood, I view 'em! I had to spank 'em. Not bout the bitch, but the principle, my nigga," Face enunciated.

"So, you let the hoe live?" World interjected quickly, his forehead crinkling.

"Ain't no way! I put the hoe in the trunk and took her to the waterfall."

"And did what?" World implored.

"Stood over her, and left her," Face pronounced, intentionally leaving the baby out of the equation.

"You shoulda put her ass in the creek! No body, no case, you know that. Shid, B3 ass too! Why you ain't put him in the creek? You left a body in my shit — nah I gotta go deal wit' deez krakaz!" World complained, shaking his head.

"I'on even know, fam. Movin' fast and shit. That's my bad, bra," Face apologized.

"The shit I do for you," World added, tapping Face on his chest. "I'ma hit'cha when I leave the station," World assured.

"Aight, 2-12," Face replied.

"2-12, bra."

Chapter 28
Almost Had 'Em

I hear you preachin' all deez raw nigga rules? You not a reverend if you made it, but can't come to the city / You not a legend / Dem jits catch you lackin' / Dey smackin' you, 911 gettin' banned from the city that made you / that's kind of heavy outside lookin' in / it's givin' they kind of jealous, but the facts is / they mad you cappin' about that steppin', they murdered all yo people / you went and bought all them weapons, let me tell you why the shit ain't work out / cause you ain't stretchin'

Face vibed to the sounds of Big Khufu's *Rawer Than You* while cutting through the city before heading to Terrell's. He blew a joint and thought about B3 and how he had put his brother in a situation that could involve prison time.

"Damn, B3. Look at what the fuck you made me do," Face mumbled under the music, stopping at a red light on 25th Street and Crane Avenue.

He took another pull from his blunt, dumped the ashes in the ashtray, and noted a vehicle approaching on his right through the rearview mirror.

"Da fuck?" Face muttered, turning the music down and grabbing his pistol.

He could see through the tint but relaxed when neither of the vehicle's windows dropped. Attempting to reach for his joint, he noticed the driver's door opened quickly with a hand clutching a pistol.

Boc! Boc! Boc! Face instinctively ducked his head and opened his door, simultaneously slipping out of the car and staying low.

Boc! Boc! Boc! Boc!

After the seventh shot, Face rose over the top of his car firing. *Boc! Boc! Boc! Boc!* The driver's and back windows shattered. Before the gunmen pulled off through the green light flushing, Face jumped back in his car and gave chase. Out of fear, the other vehicles behind veered off in opposite directions. Right when Face was nearing the BMW, he seen police lights two cars back and yanked a quick right.

"Who the fuck was that?" Face blurted out loud, his adrenaline pumping.

He reached for his blunt, lit it, then did the dash all the way to Terrell's.

***

"Fuck! I almost had that bitch-ass nigga!" G.I. yelled, banging his fist against the steering wheel.

He gripped the wheel tight and became more infuriated when noticing the bullet holes in his dashboard.

"Damn, that fuck nigga swift. I can't play wit' him," G.I. told himself as he got lost in traffic.

He had been layin' on Face ever since the incident at Assata's. Now he had caught him in traffic — and played. G.I. decided that layin' low was best.

***

When Face stepped out of the shower and into Terrell's room, she was seated on a red leather sofa that sat at the edge of her queen size bed in the nude with her legs stretched open.

Damn, this muthafucka fine, Face thought.

"Hey, baby." Terrell moaned, licking her middle and index fingers before placing them on her clit. She rotated her

146

hips and manipulated her love button in away that only a woman knew how.

"Wassup, wit it?" Face replied with nonchalance, but his dick rising told it all.

"Just playin' in this pussy, thinkin' bout'chu. I missed you so much, daddy," Terrell moaned, then turned the speed up, flicking her clit rapidly. "Aaaahh shit! Sss...ffffuck! Ummm...!" Terrell cried, cumming while rocking her pussy back and forth.

"Shit!" Face muttered, attempting to kneel in front of her to suck all the nectar from her pussy.

"Hold up!" Terrell interjected abruptly.

"Wass wrong, bae?" Face implored.

Terrell stood then kissed Face with her extremely soft lips. She turned Face around and forced him to be seated on the sofa. "After playin' in them streets; I know you need tending to. Let me ease that pressure, daddy," Terrell pronounced. kneeling in front of Face. She grabbed Face's dick and slid it in her mouth.

"Oooow, sshit!" Face moaned from the silken heat of her mouth as it slid over the head of his dick, her tongue hugging the underside. "Ffffuck," Face whispered in pure bliss as he grabbed the back of her neck and watched her sample his dick repeatedly. Unimaginable pleasure jolted throughout his body from the vice-like suction of her mouth.

"Mmmmm." Terrell moaned while eating Face like a cannibal. She sucked him so fucking slow, repeatedly forcing him to feel every swipe of her tongue and mouth.

"Fuck, you eatin' that dick up," Face cried.

Terrell took Face out of her mouth and jacked him off while using her tongue to trace an intricate patter inside of his thighs, in the crease between his leg and groin.

Between watching her suck his dick and the warmth from her mouth, Face couldn't compose himself. "Whooo, ffffuck! Ssss. Ssshit! I love you!" Face moaned, attempting to run from her touch.

"Ummhmm! Come here." Terrell moaned, deep-throating his entire dick. "Mmmmmmmm!"

Face could feel the vibrations on his dick from her moans as she picked up the pace and bobbled her head rapidly. Face thought he'd die of pleasure. "Oh my God!" Face yelled as most of the blood rushed to his erection. His body tensed up and tingles rushed up his spine while he gripped her hair with one hand and the sheets with the other. "Aaaaahhhhhggh!" Face squealed as he exploded in her mouth powerfully.

"Mmmmm…mmmm!" Terrell moaned while swallowing everything that spilled out of Face's dick.

He trembled chaotically as she sucked him dry. Even though he had just climaxed, he remained erect. Terrell took him out of her mouth, moaned while slapping his dick across her face, then rose and mounted him.

"Oh…my…fuckin'…God," Face cried while Terrell wiggled down on every inch of him.

"FFFFuck, you feel so good inside me," she moaned, gripping the back of the sofa.

Face rubbed his hands in her deep arch and rested them on her succulent butter soft ass cheeks. "Put that pussy on me," Face encouraged.

She leaned forward and started bouncing on Face's dick romantically while tongue kissing him. "Sss, ooow…I love you, daddy," she cried.

"A nigga love you, too," Face replied, grinding his hips, fucking her from the bottom, matching her rhythm perfectly.

"Sss, ooow, ffuck! I want'cho baby. Please, give me a baby, daddy," Terrell cried.

"Oh, fffuck! I'm nuttin' in this pussy!" he groaned through clenched teeth.

"Ooow, I'm nuttin' on this dick!" Terrell moaned as she switched to a slow, hard grind. Her pussy muscles clench around his shaft while she shed tears of pure pleasure.

"Fffuck, I love you, boy," Terrell asserted.

"Love you too, ma."

Chapter 29
Booked

Face made a left on 23rd and Avenue K. He crept by KoKo's mother's apartment and seen that it was empty. There had been no news of KoKo's disappearance anywhere, which led Face to believe he was in the clear.

Face pulled into B3's girlfriend's driveway, killed the engine, and got out. Ree Ree seen Face approaching and met him at the door.

"Hey, Face," Ree Ree greeted cheerfully, to Face's surprise.

"Wassup wit' it? How you doin'?" he retorted.

"Oh, I'm real good. Come in, it's hot out there," she invited.

Face stepped in, confused.

"What'chu mean, you real good?" he implored, standing in the living room.

"You talkin' bout B3, right?"

Face nodded his head.

"Yeah, I'm good. Me and B3 ain't been together for a while. I just let him do his thang until he move out, but he never did. He was doggin' me out bad, so... nall, I'm not grieving. More of a celebration, to be real," Ree Ree voiced.

"Damn! I ain't expect that. Okay then. Look, B3 had some work of mine before—"

"I already know," Ree Ree interjected. "It's back here." She waved her hand for Face to follow.

She headed to the last room on the right and entered. When Face stepped in behind her, he spotted the pounds of weed in a garbage bag that sat in the corner of the room.

"That's it, over there," she pointed.

"I know, I smell it. I appreciate'chu holdin' this shit down for me."

"Anytime," she retorted, then added: "You know he was fuckin' KoKo too, right?"

"Nawl, I ain't know that," Face lied.

"Remember when I told you if B3 wasn't here, you could get it?" Ree Ree asked, kneeling on both of her knees while slipping Face's dick from his Billionaire Boy Sweats.

"Like it was yesterday," Face retorted as his dick grew in size from her touch.

"Ummm!" Ree Ree moaned, then licked her lips, impressed with his size.

"Eat it up," Face encouraged.

She took Face's enticed dick into her mouth and throat with no gag reflex.

"Ssss…oooowww!" Face groaned, grabbing her hair.

Ree Ree took him in and out of her mouth repeatedly, slurping and sucking with purpose.

"Mmmm…mmm!" she moaned, twisting her head from left to right, gripping his dick with her left hand and massaging his balls with her right.

"Ooooo, fffuck, that dick finna skeet," Face cried through clenched teeth while standing on his toes.

Ree Ree applied more pressure, tightening her mouth up while bobbing her head rapidly.

"Aaaahhhgghhrrr!" Face exploded in Ree Ree's mouth and she swallowed every specimen.

"Mmm… you taste good," she admitted, then stood, hiking her sundress up and bending over a sofa.

Face grabbed his dick and attempted to navigate it to her love hole when his phone rang.

"Don't answer it, please! Put that dick in me, Face," she cried, waving her soft and thick ass back and forth.

Face ignored her and answered.

"Yeah?"

"Wass poppin', bra?"

"World?" Face questioned.

"Yeah, nigga, this me. Look, I'm hittin' you from Shameka phone to tell you that they booked me for B3's murder."

Shameka was their cousin who worked at the county jail.

"What!" Face snapped.

"Look, bra, don't trip. Don't say shit to nobody. I'ma take this one on the chin."

"Fuck you mean?"

"They ain't got shit on me. I'ma beat it, bra. You been through enough! I got it, nigga, and don't say shit!"

Click! World hung the phone up.

"Fffffuck!" Face yelled, putting his dick back in his sweats.

"What, baby?" Ree Ree implored.

"I gotta go," Face informed, grabbing his work before leaving.

***

After leaving Ree Ree's apartment, Face slid to his spot at the Carter to put the work up. While doing so, sporadic thoughts of who had shot at him in traffic provided his mental.

"This bitch-ass nigga," Face mumbled to himself, taking out his phone to place a call.

"Yo?" Assata answered.

"Wass poppin', gang," Face shot back.

"Niggaz like us!"

"All the time! Listen, I need to bark at'chu. You around?"

"Pull up," she proclaimed.

"Woop!" *Click!*

Face hung up, locked the spot up, and headed over to Assata's Beehive.

When he pulled up, surprisingly Assata was outside leaning over the railing on her porch, smoking a blunt. Face peaced lil Fif God and Shooter up before approaching Assata and doin' the same.

"Woop!" Face greeted.

"Woop," Assata retorted.

"Listen, the nigga I strapped up on the other day. Where he play at?"

"Why, wass poppin'?"

"I'm finna rock the boat on fool, pronto!" Face stated.

"Fool hit at me in traffic," Face added.

"How you know it was him?" Assata implored, handing the joint to Face, who quickly declined.

"When he stuck his arm out the window, he had the same Rollie on his wrist from the other day," he explained.

Assata nodded her head up and down.

"I'ma need you to give me 31 seconds on that," she insisted, meaning hold off on his get back.

"Shots been fired already, Bloody. What I'm holdin' off for?" Face implored, confused.

"I'ma handle it," she assured. "No disrespect, Damu, but I get active alone, no pressure."

"He my son's father," Assata added.

Face screwed his face up and shot her an expression that stated he didn't give a fuck if it was her son! He inhaled deeply then exhaled, changing his expression to a more understanding one.

"Aight. For you, I'll stand down," Face lied, knowing that if he caught G.I. slipping, he was gon' press play.

"Really though," she replied, meaning thank you.

"Know that I'm sayin'," Face added, meaning you welcome. "I gotta go handle some bidness, so I'ma bark at'chu later. 212, Damu," Face pronounced, peacing Assata up.

***

Face jumped in his whip and headed to Terrell's house. When he entered, she was in the kitchen cooking oxtail, mac-n-cheese, dirty rice, and sweet cornbread.

"How was your day, baby?" Terrell asked, taking the cornbread out of the oven and sitting it on top of the stove.

She then strutted over to Face, hugged his neck, then kissed him.

"It's all bad," he admitted, shaking his head in disbelief.

"What happen, daddy?" she inquired, her expression showing concern.

"My brother been detained for a body that I unalived," Face enunciated with guilt.

"Damn, baby! Do he know?"

"Yeah. I was gon' turn myself in, but he told me not to."

"That's deep. So, what's the next move?"

"Put five bands on his books, then hit up Michael A. Rosenberg," Face ordered.

"Who is he?" questioned Terrell.

"Jewish lawyer, outta Miami."

Chapter 30

It had been a whole year since Face had that shootout with G.I., and he hadn't ran across him since. There hadn't been any news of KoKo's body being found, and World had beat the murder charge after sitting nearly a year. Terrell was now four months pregnant with a baby boy, and Face couldn't have been more elated.

He was now laid up with Terrell, rubbing and kissing her stomach.

"I love you, T," Face disclosed, looking at her in her eyes.

"Love you more, daddy," she retorted, rubbing her hands through his head, massaging his scalp.

Moments later, Face's phone rang.

"Wass poppin', fam?" Face answered.

"Us, neva them," World replied. "Listen, fam, I need you to pull up to mama house," World pronounced.

"Wassup? I need to bring anything?"

"You know we stay dress to impress, but mama wanna view you," World asserted.

"Say less," Face stated.

"Face!"

"Wassup, bra?"

"A nigga love you, fool," World expressed.

"Love you too, bra," Face added. *Click!*

"Your brother?" questioned Terrell.

"Yeah. Get dressed, we goin' to my mama house," Face pronounced.

"Okay, bae."

***

I'm free at last / nigga Etta James
I wished for nights like this / Eddie Cane
Runnin' in ya bitch throat / like a heavy drain
She know my swag on a mill / You just petty change
I been a shooter / that's on eveythang
Treat'chu like my ex callin' / and let it rang

Face vibed to the sounds of Big Khufu when his phone rang. He turned the volume down and answered.

"Yeah?"

"Wass poppin', Bloody?"

"Who this?" Face replied.

"Damn, you don't know Big Slime when you hear 'em?"

"Kream?"

"The one and only, homie!"

"Aaahh! Wass barkin', homie!"

"Niggaz like us!"

"Whoop!"

"Whoop!" Kream asserted.

"Where you at, fam?"

"Oh, I'm out!"

"Yeah?"

"You already know! I'm tryna link wit'chu right nah!"

"Shid… I'm headed to my mama house, nah," Face proclaimed.

"Over there on Avenue S, ana?"

"Yeah."

"I'll meet'chu there," Kream assured.

"Aight, 2-12."

"All the time," Kream added. *Click!*

Face pulled into his mother's driveway and put the car in park.

"I'ma sit in the car for a lil minute, baby," Terrell pronounced.

"Aight. If you don't fall in there in fifteen minutes, I'ma slide back out here," he said, kissing her on the cheek and placing his pistol on the console.

"Okay, baby."

Face got out of the whip and headed inside. When Face entered the house, his mother and World were seated in the living room with odious expressions on their faces.

"Wassup? Why y'all lookin' so brazy?" Face implored.

Face felt what he knew to be the barrel of a gun placed in the back of his head.

"Hey, daddy! You miss me?"

Face knew that voice by sound. KoKo pushed the back of his head with the gun, forcing him to stumble forward.

"Sit'cho fuck-ass down, nigga!" KoKo demanded.

Face turned to face her and couldn't believe what he saw. Her face was disfigured, and she seemed to talk just a little slower than normal.

"Damn! That blik don't fuck off, ana? Bet'chu ain't suckin' all that dick nah! Pussy-ass hoe!" Face snapped.

He knew she had got the ups on him and said fuck it.

"Bra, you trippin'!" World stated with a screw face.

"Maan, fuck this hoe!" Face barked.

"Face, please," Pandora pleaded.

Face looked at his mother and toned it down.

"Nah, sit the fuck down, nigga," KoKo sneered through clenched teeth.

Face sat next to World on the couch.

"I had to learn how to walk and talk again! You left me for dead on that ditch bank, but you see, the God that I serve is a mighty one, nigga!" KoKo voiced.

"Bitch, fuck you!" Face snapped, ignoring his mother.

"Fuck me, huh?" KoKo pointed the gun at World's face.

"You remember, you spit in my face and shot the car up I was in?" she asked World.

"Look, I ain't—"

Boc!

KoKo shot World in the face, killing him instantly. Blood splattered all over Face's face and their mother's. He wiped it away slowly.

"Ffffuck!" Face yelled while looking at the hole in his brother's face.

"My son!" Pandora cried and began to tremble uncontrollably.

Face leaped at KoKo. *Boc! Boc! Boc!* She planted three hot ones in his chest, dropping him by his brother.

"Oh my God!" Pandora yelled hysterically.

"I'm sorry, mama. I had to," KoKo asserted.

Face clutched his chest and began to choke on his breath.

"Fight, baby… fight for me, please," Pandora cried, now on her knees as she began to pray.

KoKo kneeled beside Face.

"All I wanted to do was love you, nigga. You really was the only nigga who ever had my heart. Them other niggaz was just a nut. Y'all love havin' a woman at home, but fuck other bitches in the street, then got the nerve to get mad when we do it. You played a part in this toxic love-hate relationship we had. You killed my brother! Mama, did he tell you that?"

Pandora shot KoKo a look of opprobrium.

"Ffff… fffk… you bitch!" Face spat in between breaths.

KoKo shook her head in disbelief, then stood over Face.

"So, it's fuck me, huh? It's fuck me, but'chu are laid out wit' holes in ya chest, homeboy! Nawl… it's fuck you, nigga," KoKo snapped, aiming at Face's head.

"Bitch, you might as well kill me too," Pandora asserted with tears falling rapidly down her face.

"Mama, you already know what time it is."

Boc! Boc! Two hollow tips tunneled through KoKo's head, dropping her dead. Terrell walked up and stood over KoKo.

Boc! Boc! Boc! Boc! Boc! Boc! Boc! Terrell planted six more in her open face, neck, and chest, then squatted next to Face.

157

"Baby, I'm right here! Don't leave me, please! Fight, baby, the ambulance is on the way," Terrell cried, tears falling freely.

Kream walked in and saw Face stretched out, fighting for his life.

"Da fuck? Nawl, not my nigga! Bloody, I'm here wit'chu! Ya hear me? I'm here wit'chu, Blood! Fight that shit, homie!" Kream encouraged.

All type of shit flashed through Face's mind while he fought for his life. Being murdered by a woman he loved wasn't something he pictured. Everybody's words began to show up as he felt the life slipping away from his body.

"Daddy, we need you! Me and this baby need you!" Terrell cried.

Kream removed his shirt and pressed it against Face's wounds. He looked in Face's eyes and shook his head in an *I told you so* manner.

"Scratch a lover, and find a foe," Kream whispered to his bloody equal.

To Be Continued...

Lock Down Publications and Ca$h Presents
Assisted Publishing Packages

Due to an increase in the price of services we have increased our prices. The prices below reflect the price increase as of 11/1/24.

BASIC PACKAGE	UPGRADED PACKAGE
$699	**$1000**
Editing	Typing
Cover Design	Editing
Formatting	Cover Design
	Formatting
	Upload eBooks to Amazon
	Upload Paperback to Amazon
ADVANCE PACKAGE	**LDP SUPREME PACKAGE**
$1,400	**$1,700**
Typing	Typing
Editing (line editing/content)	Editing (line editing/content)
Cover Design	Cover Design
Formatting	Formatting
Copyright Registration	Copyright Registration
Proofreading	Proofreading
Upload eBooks to Amazon	Set up Amazon Account
Upload Paperback to Amazon	Upload eBooks to Amazon
	Upload Paperback to Amazon
	Advertise on LDP's Amazon and Facebook Page

***

Other services available upon request.
Additional charges may apply

Lock Down Publications
P.O. Box 944
Stockbridge, GA 30281-9998
Phone: 470 303-9761
Email: lockdownpublications@gmail.com

159

Submission Guideline

Submit the first three chapters of your completed manuscript to ldpsubmissions@gmail.com. In the subject line add **Your Book's Title**. The manuscript must be in a Word Doc file and sent as an attachment. Document should be in Times New Roman, double spaced, and in size 12 font. Also, provide your synopsis and full contact information. If sending multiple submissions, they must each be in a separate email.

Have a story but no way to send it electronically? You can still submit to LDP/Ca$h Presents. Send in the first three chapters, written or typed, of your completed manuscript to:

LDP: Submissions Dept
P.O. Box 944
Stockbridge, GA 30281-9998

DO NOT send original manuscript. Must be a duplicate.
Provide your synopsis and a cover letter containing your full contact information.

Thanks for considering LDP and Ca$h Presents.

NEW RELEASES

BLOODLINE OF A SAVAGE 1-3
THESE VICIOUS STREETS 1-3
RELENTLESS GOON 1-3
BY PRINCE A. TAUHID

THE BUTTERFLY MAFIA 1-3
BY FUMIYA PAYNE

A THUG'S STREET PRINCESS 1&2
BY MEESHA

CITY OF SMOKE 3
BY MOLOTTI

GET IT IN SLUGS 1 &2
BY B. STALL

STANDING ON HER BUSINESS 1&2
BY DG SANTANA

STEPPERS 1,2&3
THE REAL BADDIES OF CHI-RAQ
BY KING RIO

THE LANE 1&2
BY KEN-KEN SPENCE

THUG OF SPADES 1&2
LOVE IN THE TRENCHES 2
CORNER BOYS
BY COREY ROBINSON

TIL DEATH 3
BY ARYANNA

TENDER 2 | KHUFU

THE BIRTH OF A GANGSTER 4
BY DELMONT PLAYER

PRODUCT OF THE STREETS 1-3
BY DEMOND "MONEY" ANDERSON

NO TIME FOR ERROR
BY KEESE

MONEY HUNGRY DEMONS 1-2
BY TRANAY ADAMS

HUB CITY MENACE 1-3
BY J. WHITE

A THUGGISH PASSION 1&2
LAND OF DA HOOLIGANZ 1-4
KILLAZ ON STANDBY 1&2
BY IRA B.

FO'EVA ROLLIN 1&2
BY ASSA RAYMOND BAKER

THE LEVEL UP 1&3
BY LUXURY KING

Coming Soon from Lock Down Publications/Ca$h Presents

IF YOU CROSS ME ONCE 6
ANGEL V
By Anthony Fields

A THUGS STREET PRINCESS 3
By Meesha

CORNER BOYS 2
By Corey Robinson

THA TAKEOVER
By Keith Chandler

BETRAYAL OF A G 2
By Ray Vinci

SAVAGE FAMILY EMPIRE 1&2
SOULLESS GOON 1,2&3
THE DIRTY SIDE OF MONEY 1,2&3
By Prince

FOR MY ENEMY'S SAKE
AMBITIONS OF A SLIDER
FRESH OFF DA PORCH
By IRA B.

BY THE TRUCKLOAD 1-4
TIPPIN' THE SCALES 1-3
BAD BITCHES WIT GUNZ 3
PROBLEM SOLVED 2
By Christopher "Diesel" Hornezes

Available Now

RESTRAINING ORDER 1 & 2
By **CA$H & Coffee**

LOVE KNOWS NO BOUNDARIES 1-3
By **Coffee**

RAISED AS A GOON I, II, III & IV
BRED BY THE SLUMS I, II, III
BLAST FOR ME I & II
ROTTEN TO THE CORE I II III
A BRONX TALE I, II, III
DUFFLE BAG CARTEL I II III IV V VI
HEARTLESS GOON I II III IV V
A SAVAGE DOPEBOY I II
DRUG LORDS I II III
CUTTHROAT MAFIA I II
KING OF THE TRENCHES
By **Ghost**

LAY IT DOWN I & II
LAST OF A DYING BREED I II
BLOOD STAINS OF A SHOTTA I & II III
By **Jamaica**

LOYAL TO THE GAME I II III
LIFE OF SIN I, II III
By **TJ & Jelissa**

IF LOVING HIM IS WRONG…I & II
LOVE ME EVEN WHEN IT HURTS I II III
By **Jelissa**

PUSH IT TO THE LIMIT
By **Bre' Hayes**

BLOODY COMMAS I & II
SKI MASK CARTEL I, II & III
KING OF NEW YORK I II, III IV V
RISE TO POWER I II III
COKE KINGS I II III IV V
BORN HEARTLESS I II III IV
KING OF THE TRAP I II
By **T.J. Edwards**

WHEN THE STREETS CLAP BACK I & II III
THE HEART OF A SAVAGE I II III IV
MONEY MAFIA I II
LOYAL TO THE SOIL I II III
By **Jibril Williams**

A DISTINGUISHED THUG STOLE MY HEART I II & III
LOVE SHOULDN'T HURT I II III IV
RENEGADE BOYS 1-4
PAID IN KARMA 1-3
SAVAGE STORMS 1-3
AN UNFORESEEN LOVE 1-3
BABY, I'M WINTERTIME COLD 1-3
A THUG'S STREET PRINCESS 1&2
By **Meesha**

A GANGSTER'S CODE 1-3
A GANGSTER'S SYN 1-3
THE SAVAGE LIFE 1-3
CHAINED TO THE STREETS 1-3
BLOOD ON THE MONEY 1-3
A GANGSTA'S PAIN 1-3
BEAUTIFUL LIES AND UGLY TRUTHS
CHURCH IN THESE STREETS
By **J-Blunt**

CUM FOR ME 1-8
An LDP Erotica Collaboration

TENDER 2 | KHUFU

BLOOD OF A BOSS 1-5
SHADOWS OF THE GAME
TRAP BASTARD
By **Askari**

THE STREETS BLEED MURDER 1-3
THE HEART OF A GANGSTA 1-3
By **Jerry Jackson**

WHEN A GOOD GIRL GOES BAD
By **Adrienne**

THE COST OF LOYALTY 1-3
By **Kweli**

BRIDE OF A HUSTLA 1-3
THE FETTI GIRLS 1-3
CORRUPTED BY A GANGSTA 1-4
BLINDED BY HIS LOVE
THE PRICE YOU PAY FOR LOVE 1-3
DOPE GIRL MAGIC 1-3
By **Destiny Skai**

A KINGPIN'S AMBITION
A KINGPIN'S AMBITION II
I MURDER FOR THE DOUGH
By **Ambitious**

TRUE SAVAGE 1-7
DOPE BOY MAGIC 1-3
MIDNIGHT CARTEL 1-3
CITY OF KINGZ 1&2
NIGHTMARE ON SILENT AVE
THE PLUG OF LIL MEXICO 1&2
CLASSIC CITY
By **Chris Green**

TENDER 2 | KHUFU

A GANGSTER'S REVENGE 1-4
THE BOSS MAN'S DAUGHTERS 1-5
A SAVAGE LOVE 1&2
BAE BELONGS TO ME 1&2
A HUSTLER'S DECEIT 1-3
WHAT BAD BITCHES DO 1-3
SOUL OF A MONSTER 1-3
KILL ZONE
A DOPE BOY'S QUEEN 1-3
TIL DEATH 1-3
IMMA DIE BOUT MINE 1-6
DYING FOR LIKES
By **Aryanna**

A DOPEBOY'S PRAYER
By **Eddie "Wolf" Lee**

THE KING CARTEL 1-3
By **Frank Gresham**

THESE NIGGAS AIN'T LOYAL 1-3
By **Nikki Tee**

GANGSTA SHYT 1-3
By **CATO**

THE ULTIMATE BETRAYAL
By **Phoenix**

BOSS'N UP 1-3
By **Royal Nicole**

I LOVE YOU TO DEATH
By **Destiny J**

I RIDE FOR MY HITTA
I STILL RIDE FOR MY HITTA
By **Misty Holt**

TENDER 2 | KHUFU

LOVE & CHASIN' PAPER
By **Qay Crockett**

TO DIE IN VAIN
SINS OF A HUSTLA
By **ASAD**

BROOKLYN HUSTLAZ
By **Boogsy Morina**

BROOKLYN ON LOCK 1 & 2
By **Sonovia**

GANGSTA CITY
By **Teddy Duke**

A DRUG KING AND HIS DIAMOND 1-3
A DOPEMAN'S RICHES
HER MAN, MINE'S TOO 1&2
CASH MONEY HO'S
THE WIFEY I USED TO BE 1&2
PRETTY GIRLS DO NASTY THINGS
By **Nicole Goosby**

LIPSTICK KILLAH 1-3
CRIME OF PASSION 1-3
FRIEND OR FOE 1-3
By **Mimi**

TRAPHOUSE KING 1-3
KINGPIN KILLAZ 1-3
STREET KINGS 1&2
PAID IN BLOOD 1&2
CARTEL KILLAZ 1-3
DOPE GODS 1&2
By **Hood Rich**

THE STREETS ARE CALLING
By **Duquie Wilson**

TENDER 2 | KHUFU

STEADY MOBBN' 1-3
THE STREETS STAINED MY SOUL 1-3
By **Marcellus Allen**

WHO SHOT YA 1-3
SON OF A DOPE FIEND 1-4
HEAVEN GOT A GHETTO 1&2
SKI MASK MONEY 1&2
By **Renta**

GORILLAZ IN THE BAY 1-4
TEARS OF A GANGSTA 1/&2
3X KRAZY 1&2
STRAIGHT BEAST MODE 1&2
By **DE'KARI**

TRIGGADALE 1-3
MURDA WAS THE CASE 1-3
By **Elijah R. Freeman**

SLAUGHTER GANG 1-3
RUTHLESS HEART 1-3
By **Willie Slaughter**

GOD BLESS THE TRAPPERS 1-3
THESE SCANDALOUS STREETS 1-3
FEAR MY GANGSTA 1-5
THESE STREETS DON'T LOVE NOBODY 1-2
BURY ME A G 1-5
A GANGSTA'S EMPIRE 1-4
THE DOPEMAN'S BODYGAURD 1&2
THE REALEST KILLAZ 1-3
THE LAST OF THE OGS 1-3
By **Tranay Adams**

MARRIED TO A BOSS 1-3
By **Destiny Skai & Chris Green**

169

KINGZ OF THE GAME 1-7
CRIME BOSS 1-4
By **Playa Ray**

FUK SHYT
By **Blakk Diamond**

DON'T F#CK WITH MY HEART 1&2
By **Linnea**

ADDICTED TO THE DRAMA 1-3
IN THE ARM OF HIS BOSS
By **Jamila**

LOYALTY AIN'T PROMISED 1&2
By **Keith Williams**

YAYO 1-4
A SHOOTER'S AMBITION 1&2
BRED IN THE GAME
By **S. Allen**

TRAP GOD 1-3
RICH $AVAGE 1-3
MONEY IN THE GRAVE 1-3
CARTEL MONEY 1&2
By **Martell Troublesome Bolden**

FOREVER GANGSTA 1&2
GLOCKS ON SATIN SHEETS 1&2
By **Adrian Dulan**

TOE TAGZ 1-4
LEVELS TO THIS SHYT 1&2
IT'S JUST ME AND YOU
By **Ah'Million**

KINGPIN DREAMS 1-3
RAN OFF ON DA PLUG
By **Paper Boi Rari**

THE STREETS MADE ME 1-3
By **Larry D. Wright**

CONFESSIONS OF A GANGSTA 1-4
CONFESSIONS OF A JACKBOY 1-3
CONFESSIONS OF A HITMAN
CONFESSIONS OF A DOPE BOY
By **Nicholas Lock**

I'M NOTHING WITHOUT HIS LOVE
SINS OF A THUG
TO THE THUG I LOVED BEFORE
A GANGSTA SAVED XMAS
IN A HUSTLER I TRUST
By **Monet Dragun**

QUIET MONEY 1-3
THUG LIFE 1-3
EXTENDED CLIP 1&2
A GANGSTA'S PARADISE
By **Trai'Quan**

CAUGHT UP IN THE LIFE 1-3
THE STREETS NEVER LET GO 1-3
By **Robert Baptiste**

NEW TO THE GAME 1-3
MONEY, MURDER & MEMORIES 1-3
By **Malik D. Rice**

CREAM 2-3
THE STREETS WILL TALK
By **Yolanda Moore**

THE STREETS WILL NEVER CLOSE 1-3
By **K'ajji**

LIFE OF A SAVAGE 1-4
A GANGSTA'S QUR'AN 1-4
MURDA SEASON 1-3
GANGLAND CARTEL 1-3
CHI'RAQ GANGSTAS 1-4
KILLERS ON ELM STREET 1-3
JACK BOYZ N DA BRONX 1-3
A DOPEBOY'S DREAM 1-3
JACK BOYS VS DOPE BOYS 1-3
COKE GIRLZ
COKE BOYS
SOSA GANG 1&2
BRONX SAVAGES
BODYMORE KINGPINS
BLOOD OF A GOON
By **Romell Tukes**

CONCRETE KILLA 1-3
VICIOUS LOYALTY 1-3
BLOODY MONEY BAGS
By **Kingpen**

THE ULTIMATE SACRIFICE 1-6
KHADIFI
IF YOU CROSS ME ONCE 1-3
ANGEL 1-4
IN THE BLINK OF AN EYE
By **Anthony Fields**

THE LIFE OF A HOOD STAR
By **Ca$h & Rashia Wilson**

NIGHTMARES OF A HUSTLA 1-3
BLOOD AND GAMES 1&2
By **King Dream**

GHOST MOB
By **Stilloan Robinson**

HARD AND RUTHLESS 1&2
MOB TOWN 251
THE BILLIONAIRE BENTLEYS 1-3
REAL G'S MOVE IN SILENCE
By **Von Diesel**

MOB TIES 1-7
SOUL OF A HUSTLER, HEART OF A KILLER 1-3
GORILLAZ IN THE TRENCHES
OOPS CRY TOO 1&2
THE DAUGHTER OF A CARTEL BOSS
By **SayNoMore**

BODYMORE MURDERLAND 1-3
THE BIRTH OF A GANGSTER 1-4
By **Delmont Player**

FOR THE LOVE OF A BOSS 1&2
By **C. D. Blue**

KILLA KOUNTY 1-5
TENDER
By **Khufu**

MOBBED UP 1-4
THE BRICK MAN 1-5
THE COCAINE PRINCESS 1-10
STEPPERS 1-3
SUPER GREMLIN 1-4
A GANGSTA'S SON
By **King Rio**

MONEY GAME 1&2
By **Smoove Dolla**

TENDER 2 | KHUFU

A GANGSTA'S KARMA 1-5
By **FLAME**

KING OF THE TRENCHES 1-3
By **GHOST & TRANAY ADAMS**

BAD BITCHES WIT GUNZ 1&2
PROBLEM SOLVED
By **"Christopher Diesel" Hornezes**

QUEEN OF THE ZOO 1&2
By **Black Migo**

GRIMEY WAYS 1-3
BETRAYAL OF A G
By **Ray Vinci**

XMAS WITH AN ATL SHOOTER
By **Ca$h & Destiny Skai**

KING KILLA 1&2
By **Vincent "Vitto" Holloway**

BETRAYAL OF A THUG 1&2
By **Fre$h**

COUNTDOWN OF A KILLA 1&2
SEX, MURDER AND GOD 1&2
GUNS DOWN, BOTTOMS UP 1&2
By Lo-Life

THE MURDER QUEENS 1-7
By **Michael Gallon**

FOR THE LOVE OF BLOOD 1-4
By **Jamel Mitchell**

TENDER 2 | KHUFU

HOOD CONSIGLIERE 1&2
NO TIME FOR ERROR
By **Keese**

PROTÉGÉ OF A LEGEND 1,2&3
LOVE IN THE TRENCHES 1&2
By **Corey Robinson**

THE PLUG'S RUTHLESS DAUGHTER 1&2
By **Tony Daniels**

BORN IN THE GRAVE 1-3
CRIME PAYS
By **Self Made Tay**

MOAN IN MY MOUTH
By **XTASY**

TORN BETWEEN A GANGSTER AND A GENTLEMAN
By **J-BLUNT & Miss Kim**

LOYALTY IS EVERYTHING 1-3
CITY OF SMOKE 1-3
By **Molotti**

HERE TODAY GONE TOMORROW 1&2
By **Fly Rock**

WOMEN LIE MEN LIE 1-4
FIFTY SHADES OF SNOW 1-3
STACK BEFORE YOU SPLURGE
GIRLS FALL LIKE DOMINOES
NAÏVE TO THE STREETS
By **ROY MILLIGAN**

PILLOW PRINCESS
By **S. Hawkins**

THE BUTTERFLY MAFIA 1-3
SALUTE MY SAVAGERY 1&2
By **Fumiya Payne**

THE LANE 1&2
By Ken-Ken Spence

THE PUSSY TRAP 1-5
By **Nene Capri**

DIRTY DNA
By **Blaque**

SANCTIFIED AND HORNY
by **XTASY**

BOOKS BY LDP'S CEO, CA$H

TRUST IN NO MAN
TRUST IN NO MAN 2
TRUST IN NO MAN 3
BONDED BY BLOOD
SHORTY GOT A THUG
THUGS CRY
THUGS CRY 2
THUGS CRY 3
TRUST NO BITCH
TRUST NO BITCH 2
TRUST NO BITCH 3
TIL MY CASKET DROPS
RESTRAINING ORDER
RESTRAINING ORDER 2
IN LOVE WITH A CONVICT
LIFE OF A HOOD STAR
XMAS WITH AN ATL SHOOTER